Sword Art Online Alternative GUN GALE ONLINE V

3rd Squad Jam: Betrayers' Choice: Finish

Keiichi Sigsawa

ILLUSTRATION BY
Kouhaku Kuroboshi

SUPERVISED BY
Reki Kawahara

NEW YORK

SWORD ART ONLINE Alternative Gun Gale Online, Vol. 5
KEIICHI SIGSAWA

Translation by Stephen Paul
Cover art by Kouhaku Kuroboshi

SWORD ART ONLINE Alternative Gun Gale Online Vol. V
©KEIICHI SIGSAWA / REKI KAWAHARA 2016
First published in Japan in 2016 by KADOKAWA CORPORATION, Tokyo.
English translation rights arranged with KADOKAWA CORPORATION, Tokyo, through TUTTLE-MORI AGENCY, INC., Tokyo.

English translation © 2019 by Yen Press, LLC

Yen On
150 West 30th Street, 19th Floor
New York, NY 10001

Visit us at yenpress.com
facebook.com/yenpress
twitter.com/yenpress
yenpress.tumblr.com
instagram.com/yenpress

First Yen On Edition: November 2019

Yen On is an imprint of Yen Press, LLC.
The Yen On name and logo are trademarks of Yen Press, LLC.

Library of Congress Cataloging-in-Publication Data
Names: Sigsawa, Keiichi, 1972– author. | Kuroboshi, Kōhaku, illustrator. |
    Kawahara, Reki, supervisor. | Paul, Stephen (Translator), translator.
Title: Third Squad Jam : betrayers' choice: finish / Keiichi Sigsawa ; illustration by
    Kouhaku Kuroboshi ; supervised by Reki Kawahara ; translation by Stephen Paul.
Description: New York, NY : Yen On, 2019. | Series: Sword art online alternative
    gun gale online ; Volume 5
Identifiers: LCCN 2019038622 | ISBN 9781975353872 (trade paperback)
Subjects: CYAC: Fantasy games—Fiction. | Virtual reality—Fiction. |
    Role playing—Fiction.
Classification: LCC PZ7.1.S537 Thi 2019 | DDC [Fic]—dc23
LC record available at https://lccn.loc.gov/2019038622

ISBNs: 978-1-9753-5387-2 (paperback)
        978-1-9753-5393-3 (ebook)

10 9 8 7 6 5 4 3 2 1

LSC-C

Printed in the United States of America

Early summer, 2026.

   The battle to save Pitohui's life in the second Squad Jam ends safely, and Karen Kohiruimaki returns to an uneventful college life. Then she gets word of the upcoming third Squad Jam…

   Llenn refuses to log in because she doesn't want to fight Pitohui again. But when Pitohui suggests they be teammates so Llenn can fulfill her promise to have a rematch with Team SHINC, Llenn reluctantly agrees to enter SJ3.

   Thus, LPFM was born, a powerhouse team including Fukaziroh and M. But the rules of SJ3 are extreme.

The battlefield is slowly sinking into the sea. An area labeled UNKNOWN lies in the center of the map. And there is a special rule that will only be revealed and come into play by the middle stages of the battle…

"The players who are named will leave their teams as betrayers. All listed betrayers will form a new team and fight on the same side."

Team LPFM's betrayer ends up being none other than the last person Llenn wants to fight: Pitohui.

CHAPTER 8

SECT.8

What SHINC Was Doing

CHAPTER 8
What SHINC Was Doing

July 5th, 2026.

12:03 PM.

"Bwa-ha-ha-ha!" Boss let out a tremendous belly laugh.

She stared down the approaching sea at the southeast corner of the island.

"Very good! We've got a fire lit under our asses, ladies! We're gonna charge straight through all this nonsense: No stopping! No mercy!"

When the game started three minutes earlier, SHINC was on the shoreline of the island's southeast corner.

According to the unwritten rule established in SJ2, the toughest teams were spread to the four corners. So they were at a great distance from the previous champions, T-S, as well as MMTM and Llenn's team.

A wasteland of huge rock pillars lay around them. The structures were between fifty and seventy feet tall, and fifteen feet across, sprouting up across the landscape at intervals of a hundred feet or two.

As M suspected, this eerie series of formations, which looked like a gang of monstrous mushrooms, was a bit of natural art created through rain erosion. The water pounded softer earth, and only the spots where a different vein of tougher rock was on top remained, until they stood like towers.

The ground layer beneath them was hard rock, and it was essentially flat, so there was no place to hide except behind the towers. But since SHINC knew that no team would be within exactly one kilometer at the start of the game, they were safe for now—and the field of rocks kept them hidden from long-distance attacks. The six members of their team warily eyed the land around them and picked out a good spot to watch the 12:10 Satellite Scan come in.

But after only the first minute, Tanya, the small and agile point person, cried out, "Hey! The sea! The sea's creeping up on us!"

She had noticed the special nature of the map: that either the island was sinking or the sea was rising—and that the available space would shrink over time.

Implicitly understanding the intentions of the designer, Boss let out a belly laugh and immediately changed plans.

"Oh?"

The crowd watching the event on the monitors in the pub noticed quickly that SHINC was engaging in a bold new strategy.

Everyone, participants and audience alike, knew that there was no need to go on the offensive in the first ten minutes. So it was widely expected that the fighting would only commence once the initial Satellite Scan at 12:10 was over.

The crowd was taking it easy. They ate and drank, chatting with their friends about who they expected to win it all. When the large monitors hanging from the ceiling showed SHINC had burst into top speed, they were stunned.

"Huh? They started charging outta nowhere."

"What? It just started!"

On the screen, little Tanya with her Bizon submachine gun was leading the charge, with all six of them at a full sprint.

"What's going on? What are they thinking?"

"Are they desperate because they noticed the tide coming in?"

"The top contenders? No way."

As they watched, mystified and slightly nervous, the members of SHINC began traveling from one rock pillar to the next, guns held at the waist, with the sea on their left. They sped along smoothly, without hesitation.

Tanya was far faster than the others, so at times, she would stop to check the area while she waited for the rest to catch up, but they kept moving without any breaks.

After two minutes and change, the clock on the side of the monitor display showed that it was 12:05, and the women came to an abrupt stop. They'd run several hundred yards at least, going by what Tanya mouthed on the screen—there wasn't any audio.

Instantly, the group hid behind the pillars, except for Anna, the rear guard, who started a laborious climb up the rock before her. She was free climbing without any ropes, a rather treacherous activity, as the handholds weren't exactly big. Her agility was impressive.

"That's wild. I bet she's got to have some kind of Climbing skill," one of the audience members said with great confidence, but he was wrong. It was not a character skill, but a *player* skill— specifically, that of Moe Annaka, Anna's player. She'd been forced to take part in her parents' hobby of bouldering from a young age.

In fact, all of Team SHINC, not just Moe, were young athletes.

They exercised and performed athletic feats every single day, so unlike the out-of-shape gamers who only played heroes and warriors online, their fundamental physical coordination was rock-solid.

Anna quickly hauled herself upward, her blond hair and Dragunov rifle swaying with each movement. When she had finished climbing the five-story-tall rock, an easy task for her, she arranged her body so that she was lying down flat on its top. She shrugged the Dragunov off her back and to the right, then took out a pair of binoculars and began to search.

Within five seconds, Anna muttered something and switched to her rifle.

Without getting up, she took aim and fired the first shot of SJ3.

"Whyyyy meee?" groaned the first casualty of SJ3 as he departed the mortal plane. Despite the fierce wind, Anna emerged victorious.

Her very first shot hit him in the chest. The second one went through his forehead. The unlucky insta-kill.

The man's muscular body fell smack against the rocky earth, sending up the smallest of dust clouds. His upright Mohawk was now flat on the ground.

Naturally, his teammates jumped up in alarm. They stood fifteen feet away, looking around cautiously.

"Huh? What? Hey? Why?"

"Is this a joke?"

"Get down!" someone shouted. Ducking for cover was about all they could do.

Their displayed team tag was BKA. They were a squadron that often played *Gun Gale Online* together, and their team's chief characteristic—or concept, or theme—was postapocalyptic.

There was a famous old movie about violent roving gangs in a post-nuclear collapse, roaring and raucous—as well as a famous old kung-fu manga inspired by that film series. This group was dedicated to re-creating that way of life in the game, and it started with their outfits.

Some wore tattered leather jackets with heavy protective patches, some wore no shirts and painted their bare skin odd colors, some (like the one who just died) styled their hair in punk Mohawks, and some smeared intimidating face paint on their cheeks.

Their guns, too, were chosen to be as dated and as primitive as possible, all of them from the 1970s or older. They even customized the guns with mud and grime and broken parts, in some cases even combining multiple guns into a new chimera firearm. The AK-47 of the dead Mohawk man featured a trowel handle for a stock, for example.

They took their "madness to the maximum" in pursuit of the aesthetic. If there were group pictures of each squad in SJ3, they might come out on top in terms of sheer visual impact.

As a matter of fact, this team of fearsome wasteland warriors, designed to make children everywhere cry, was actually made up of friendly kindergarten teachers, local firefighters, and cram school teachers popular with middle school girls.

"Oh, the poor things…"

The members of BKA received nothing but glances of pity from the audience in the pub. It was easy to envision them all dying in short order on the live feed.

Once Anna had spotted them and abruptly taken out the first one, her follow-up semiauto sniping forced the rest to either hit the dirt or hide behind a nearby pillar.

And once they did, the rest of the women were merciless.

With her high vantage point, Anna could report to the other members of the team on the location of the enemy. She also knew that no other squads were nearby.

There was only one thing to do: wipe them out.

Silver-haired Tanya shot forward like the wind, flanking the enemy team from the right. Her gun soon found a topless macho man hiding behind a rock pillar. He was no more than a hundred feet away. He had his head down, fearful of being sniped, and didn't even see her.

But Tanya didn't shoot him right away. She kept her aim steady and waited, speaking to her teammates through her communication device. Ten seconds later, the roar of a PKM machine gun started up. The heavy percussion of its fire echoed powerfully through the dry environment.

A merciless storm of bullets descended upon the hiding spot of the postapocalyptic team between the pillars of rock. A number of them took hits, but it wasn't enough to be fatal, so all five survivors took off running.

An ironclad rule of battle in *GGO* was that if the enemy had a bead on you, and you knew your position was exposed, you had to run away at full speed. Tucking your tail between your legs wasn't a shameful act. As long as you still had hit points left, you could recover and fight again.

But sadly for them, they could not hear the voice of the audience member, who could see the situation quite clearly, say "Oh, don't run *that* way."

The five men sprouted damage effects all over their bodies like flowers, visual indicators of being shot, and toppled over one after the other. These bullets had come from Tanya's Bizon, which was trained on them all along, and from Boss's Vintorez as she caught up.

They shot down the five fleeing men as if this were easy target practice.

It wouldn't be until after the first team to get knocked out of SJ3 had a chance to see the recorded footage that they would realize the initial PKM fire was only meant to lure them into a trap.

By 12:09, SHINC had already knocked out one competitor before the first scan even started.

"Those chicks are crazy."

"They're definitely not the sweet type...," the audience in the pub declared in a mixture of admiration and intimidation.

"I'll watch the scan! Everyone keep an eye out!" Boss commanded, her voice crisp and clear. The other women formed a circle. Not an inward-facing one, but a deadly outward circle with eyes alert and guns at the ready.

The five of them kept a 360-degree watch on the world of pillars around them. It was possible that another squad nearby knew they were here from only the sound, before any Satellite Scan entered into it.

Each member was lying down on the dirt at least fifteen feet from her nearest partner, to ensure they couldn't all be blown up with a single grenade. Each of them held her own gun at the ready, except for Sophie, who was in charge of hauling.

Only Boss looked at her Satellite Scan terminal.

12:10.

The first Satellite Scan of the third Squad Jam had begun.

"Everyone head north-northeast! One thousand yards!" Boss commanded ten seconds later, stashing her device back in her pocket. The women leaped to their feet and resumed sprinting.

Not a single one of the group was slacking off. They were precise, disciplined, and focused.

But the scan was still ongoing. That meant Boss gave her orders knowing full well that all the other teams would see the way they were moving across the map as it happened. Still, her teammates followed her words with absolute trust.

Without warning, a yellow flare shot up into the sky in the direction the six women raced.

"Wh-what…?" Boss stammered, eyes wide. But she soon broke into a wild grin and roared, "Yes! So that's the strategy! Perfect! They'll be the next target! Let's go kill 'em all!"

"See, that's a signal that they're all going to gang up on the tougher teams," said an audience member wearing a beret. As the crowd watched Llenn's squad on the monitors, the spectator started to launch into a cocky speech about how the groups were going to team up, but he didn't get far.

"Whoa, they're already rushing off for the next one?!" shouted the audience for SHINC's footage. They didn't particularly care to hear about the meaning of the yellow flare.

Not when the next battle was on.

*   *   *

"They're already charging us!"

"I don't believe it!" the men practically shrieked, tossing aside their terminals and picking up their guns. They pointed them in a south-southwest direction.

Both carried large MG 2504 machine guns, which were a good four feet long.

Another member had a Sorpressa A2 sniper rifle, which stood out for having such a huge, powerful scope that its slim barrel looked like the attachment, not the other way around.

The other three used G991K assault rifles, more compact at about three feet long.

If the names didn't sound familiar, that was for good reason: They were all fictional optical guns.

"Fire! Full assault!"

The guns began emitting not the percussive sounds of gunfire blasts, but crisp energy emissions that more resembled the chittering of birds.

A viewer of SJ2 might have recognized the team on the screen who had just begun shooting. They were the team who took up a position in the train station in the town at the northwest part of the map.

Their team tag was RGB.

It looked at a glance like a red-green-blue abbreviation, but no. It stood for Ray Gun Boys.

Between the jeans, the full-body camo, and the sci-fi-style work uniforms, the members were decked out in a wide variety of clothing, but they had one very strict policy when it came to weapons.

As the ray gun name suggested, every member in the squadron used one of the fictional optical guns of *GGO*. They were futuristic weapons said to have come back with humanity on a spaceship, while the live-ammo guns were either relics of Earth's past or re-created from design documents.

Optical guns fired projectiles of light supplied by energy packs. Setting aside how they actually worked, they were quite excellent weapons, with many advantages.

For one thing, the guns themselves were light, so there was less concern about weight limits and movement limits. The MG 2504 was an excellent example; it was the size of a regular machine gun, but it weighed nearly half as much, at barely ten pounds. Other optical guns would be about two-thirds the weight of their counterparts.

Also, its user could fire a great many shots from a single energy pack. The exact number depended on the capacity of the pack and the power of a single shot, so it all depended on the energy cost of the gun, but even small pistols could hold a hundred per pack. Most machine guns could shoot nearly a thousand times in succession before needing a fresh one.

On top of that, while live bullets were subject to the forces of wind and gravity, an optical gun had much higher precision for long-range sniping, and because every shot glowed with light, it was easy to adjust future shots to correct your aim.

But naturally, the disadvantages were equally severe:

They were less powerful in poor weather conditions like rain and fog.

The gun fanatics who played *GGO* didn't really enjoy the fictional designs.

The lack of recoil helped firing accuracy, but it also made the shooting feedback feel underwhelming. Some people said it was like shooting air guns.

But the biggest drawback of all was that their power could be significantly curtailed in player-on-player combat with an anti-optical defense field—an item that everyone owned.

They were fully effective on monsters in the wilderness, however, so the expert players of *GGO* learned to switch around their usage effectively as the situation required.

Naturally, in a pure PvP situation like Squad Jam, it made no sense to use optical guns, but Team RGB went out of their way to incorporate them.

"We're gonna show everyone the beauty of optical guns! Soon enough you'll all be copying us!"

"The price of these guns is gonna go up. Should we buy stock in optical gun makers?"

"Who cares if they're worse? Overcoming that handicap is what will make us truly shine! As bright as our bullets!" they crowed.

When they took part in SJ2, as those viewers might again recall, they lasted as long as it took Fukaziroh to bombard them with grenades and lost without doing anything notable.

Now they were in SJ3. And as the man in the beret at the bar had explained to them, they fired up a yellow flare as soon as the first scan came in.

"Why are they charging right for us?!"

Not realizing that it was only calling the bloodthirsty Amazons of Team SHINC down upon them.

"Already onto the next battle? The tempo's too fast!"

"Who cares? It means we don't get bored watching!" cheered the crowd.

Displayed on the monitor, Team RGB began shooting. They'd brought tons of energy packs with them and were firing as though running out of ammo was the last worry on their minds.

Six optical muzzles flashed. They sprayed light as generously as water from a hose.

The shots were yellow, light green, and orange. Players could customize the color at will, so this particular team chose to coordinate by gun type: yellow for machine gun, green for assault rifle, and orange for sniper rifle.

The exit velocity of a light round upon leaving the gun was essentially the same as a live bullet, but it did not lose velocity from air resistance. Instead, the amount of damage inflicted decreased with distance.

The glowing shots blazed between the towers of rock until

they reached the midst of SHINC, about two thousand feet away—where a number of them hit their targets.

On the screen, the audience saw several glowing-yellow trails heading straight for Boss's sizable body as she ran head-on.

Splish! Splish!

The shining lights shrank and crumbled right before they got to her, with little splashing sounds.

"Wow, that didn't do any damage at all..."

"Well, not at *that* range," the audience lamented.

That was the power of the anti-optical defense field, a must-have item for every *GGO* player. It created an invisible cocoon around any person who equipped it, minimizing the power of the optical rounds, no matter the angle.

Its defensive power depended on the distance of the shot but given that SHINC was at least seven hundred yards away, the numerical damage the bullets inflicted was miniscule.

"We can do it! We're hitting 'em! Keep shooting!"

Even still, the men of RGB were fired up.

"Yeah!"

"Let's do it!"

"You bet!"

The sight of tricolor laser fire stretching into the distance was a beautiful one. There'd be no fireworks show like this with real guns without exclusively using tracer rounds that lit up to show their trajectory.

"We shot off the flare! If we just hold out in this spot, others will come to help!"

They weren't simply trigger-happy idiots. There was a formula for victory in mind. SHINC's abrupt charge came as a shock to them, but they trusted that their position was solid and would lead them to triumph.

When other teams saw SHINC's location on the scan and then the yellow flare in the sky, they would rush over to join the fight. The members of RBG could see no downside to this plan.

They merely had to hold out and survive for a few minutes until help arrived. Fortunately for them, they used optical guns with little concern over ammo. They didn't need to knock out their opponent at this distance; they just needed to keep them at bay.

Even with the defensive fields, the damage inflicted would rise as they got closer, so SHINC wasn't simply going to charge blindly at them. They might run away instead, but if that happened, RGB could just wait for the other squads to show up before going after them.

In other words, they were intentionally creating a stalemate situation that was to their own benefit.

"We can do this! Fire, fire, fiiiire!"

"Roger thaaaat!"

Their smiles shone as brightly as their laser rounds.

The shower of optical rounds descended upon Boss, erasing their red bullet lines as they went, but—*splish, splish*—she ignored them entirely. It was damaging her hit point total, but not enough to care about at this point.

She took her time walking from side to side, peering through binoculars, counting "One, two, three…four, five, six!"

The points she was counting were brighter than the bullets or the lines—they were the sources of the shining light projectiles themselves. In other words, around the pillars in between, she could see every last member of the enemy squad.

Boss lowered the binoculars with a smile that needed to be kept as far from any children as possible. She ordered her companions, "Bring out the fang, girls!"

"Exchanging pack!" called out one of the RGB members to his teammates. They'd been firing so fast and frequently that even the optical gun's ammo was running out.

"You got it!" a teammate replied. No matter what kind of gun players used, the team's overall firepower lowered when they were out of ammo, so a part of teamwork was letting the others know when that was going to happen.

With a live-ammo gun, people called out something like "Reloading!" but since this was an optical gun, they said "Exchanging!"

The man pressed a button in the middle of the machine gun resting in front of him. A thick box about the size of a phone book plopped out of the bottom. It was dark gray and made of a strange material that seemed like both metal and plastic. That was the energy pack.

Energy packs could be recharged at stores, so people didn't discard one without a good reason out in the wilderness, but in Squad Jam, it didn't matter. Once the event was over, any item a player dropped, as long as it wasn't broken, automatically returned to their inventory. Even regular ammunition was subject to this rule.

The man pulled a fresh pack out of a pouch on his left side and jammed it into the top of the machine gun. It slid in smoothly and locked into place. With a pleasing little whirr, the digital indicator on the top of the gun lit up and showed nine hundred shots left. The ease of reloading was one of the benefits of optical guns.

"The optical age is upon us!" the man crowed, like some kind of forward-thinking pioneer, and he pointed the muzzle at SHINC again. "Raaaaah!"

The moment he started to unleash a withering storm of fully automatic laser fire was also the moment his head came off, and he died.

In the instant of death, the player's avatar froze in place, so his grip on the machine gun was intact, leaving it firing on its own. Two seconds later, his headless body toppled backward, pulling the gun upward to shoot directly into the sky.

"What's up? You hunting birds now, dude?" joked one of his teammates when he noticed the change in aim. The man was on the ground in firing position with an assault rifle, and he briefly stopped shooting and glanced over long enough to scream "*Fwaaieieaiah!*"

All he saw was the headless body of his buddy, shooting wildly up into the sky.

The next moment, a massive projectile split his rifle in two, continued to his chest, and burst through the back end.

"Two down. Nice work, keep going," Boss said, peering through her binoculars as she stood boldly, feet planted shoulder-width apart. An optical round *splish*ed in front of her, and she ignored the fraction of a percent of damage it did to her.

A few yards to her side sat Sophie, the squat, dwarflike woman. In a cross-legged pose, she was practically another rock on the ground. And over the left shoulder of that rock rested a huge metal pipe.

The nearly four-foot pipe had its own grip and stock, which black-haired Tohma kept propped against her own shoulder.

"They're already using that?!"

"Here comes the Degtyaryov!" roared the gun freaks in the crowd—that described nearly all *GGO* players, though.

This gun was SHINC's horrific secret weapon from the last event: the PTRD-41 anti-tank rifle, high school girls' gymnastics team special.

The PTRD-41 was the greatest possible offensive weapon, which SHINC cleared an ultra-difficult quest to obtain, all for the purpose of destroying M's shield in SJ2. Naturally, they'd brought it into SJ3 as well.

A 14.5 mm barrel, a stunningly long and heavy gun, at over six feet in length and thirty-five pounds. Naturally, it was completely obnoxious to carry around, too.

Like last time, Sophie kept her PKM machine gun and ammo in her inventory and only brought them out when she needed to use them, to ensure that she could use this anti-tank gun whenever convenient.

The downside was that if Sophie died in combat, no one else

could use it. So the team prioritized her survival most of all, even over Boss's.

It was up to the black-haired Tohma, the best shot on the team, to actually fire the rifle. In SJ1, she had succeeded in hitting tiny Llenn with her first shot from six hundred yards away, using a Dragunov that was hardly the best among sniper rifles when it came to accuracy.

Tohma kept the gun on Sophie's shoulder as a base as she quickly jammed the next huge bullet into the middle of the rifle. She slammed the long, thick bolt forward, after the force of the shot had launched it back, and pulled it down to lock it in.

With the reloading complete, Tohma jammed one knee to the ground, pressed her eye to the scope, and fine-tuned her aim.

In the meantime, RGB's optical rounds were flying at the two of them, but from the angles caught by the live feed, they weren't intimidated by that—if anything, they were smiling.

Someone in the crowd noted, "No, wait...the Amazons have the advantage! They just have to aim at where all the bright light is coming from."

"Ooh, good point!"

Indeed, that was Boss's strategy. Because the optical guns were shooting projectiles of light itself, it was unavoidable that the muzzle flash from the guns would be very noticeable. She had picked out that particular spot to stop because she was able to see six different sources of flashing at once. If they set up the PTRD-41 there, they could shoot at any one of the enemy soldiers.

Tohma fired for a third time, the blast echoing all the way to the interior of the distant pub. A two-ounce slug of metal rocketed forward at three times the speed of sound, tearing through the backdrop of laser beams toward the blinking lights that were their source.

"Don't hold back! Keep shoot—"

Those were the last words of the third member of RGB to die.

Tohma's bullet line was visible against his body, but he was so absorbed in the light show of his own machine gun that he failed to notice it. And so another member fell.

"No way... Are you kidding me...?"

In fact, make that two.

The bullet blasted through the man, obliterating him from left breast to shoulder, and continued onward to hit the neck of the man passing behind him in a crouch.

The second man's hit points shot downward with the glowing bullet-wound effect on the right side of his neck. Since the carotid artery was in the neck, even a small bullet could be fatal if it struck the right spot.

"Huh? W-wait..."

He lifted his hands to press against his neck, but that was not going to help a ruptured artery. The game system determined that he had lost too much blood and changed his status to dead.

The man toppled backward like a log, and a marker reading DEAD appeared over his corpse.

"Dammit!"

"Is anyone showing up yet?"

The two surviving members of RGB crouched behind one of the rock towers, continuing to shoot and harass their attackers. They held out for most of another minute, until one of them took a shot from the PTRD-41 that was so powerful, it broke through his rock cover to hit him and destroyed his assault rifle in the process.

"Gahk!"

But he wasn't giving up yet. He boldly leaped up to grab a weapon left behind by one of his dead teammates.

"Gah!"

But Anna's Dragunov bullets hit him in the leg, then the stomach, then the head. His SJ3 run was over.

The last member continued to fight.

"C'mon! Come get some if you dare, bitches!" he swore, moving quickly and erratically to avoid being sniped. He shot his machine gun from the waist until he needed to switch packs, then started up again, until—

"Here I am."

Tanya was suddenly right in his vicinity, having raced unseen from rock to rock toward his position.

"Huh? No way... You're so close! *Blugh!*"

She put over twenty 9 mm bullets into his back and killed him.

It was after 12:13 at that moment. From start to finish, the battle had taken no more than three minutes.

"No enemies in sight! Now, to loot the bodies," said Tanya after she briefly surveyed the horizon. She reached for the man's corpse.

On the monitor, the crowd watched the silver-haired woman searching the brand-new body.

"Huh? What's she doing?" one man asked, stunned. "Is she taking the optical guns? I mean, I guess you *can* do that until the end of the event."

"I heard they stole their defeated opponents' comms in SJ2 and used them to communicate with Llenn—or something. Maybe they'll do the same thing again."

"Do you think they're setting up a grenade booby trap to catch anyone who might be thinking of the same idea? That way, if someone tries to loot the body, it'll explode!"

"Or maybe she's just molesting his body because she can't get any male attention in real life..."

The crowd had a variety of rather imaginative answers, but the footage quickly made it clear that every last one of them was wrong.

Tanya stood up, stepped away from the man's body, and promptly fired a yellow flare signal upward.

"Ohhh!" shouted a man who'd been listening to the speech of the fellow in the red beret earlier. His recognition of the flare strategy made him so excited that he spilled most of his drink.

"What? What's that mean?"

"Yeah, what's the deal with the flares?" the other audience members asked, turning to him.

The first man explained what he'd just learned about the flares: They were a gathering signal for the weaker teams to congregate around in order to fight the main contenders. The yellow flares were meant to indicate the presence of SHINC.

"Oh! So that's what it means!"

"Wow, that's pretty clever…"

And of course, the people enthusiastic enough about *GGO* to congregate and watch this event were also smart enough to intuit what Tanya was doing by pulling the flare off a dead man to shoot it.

"I did it! There's lots of them left, too!" Tanya chirped into the comm. Behind the rock pillar, Boss smiled to herself. She had a frightening face, but once she smiled, it became apparent that—actually, her smile was frightening, too.

Behind her, four teammates watched the area warily, including Sophie, who was hauling the PTRD-41. They were the eyes of predators looking for the next throat to rip open.

"Okay, the next flare will go up in thirty seconds. Shoot that from about five hundred yards to the east of us."

"Thirty seconds! Five hundred east! Roger that!"

Boss was only giving orders to Tanya, but it was enough for the other four to know their instructions, too. Without another word, they headed east with guns at the ready.

From that point on, SHINC thoroughly dismantled each enemy squad who came for them.

They shot up the flares they stole, luring in enemies who thought *Hey, let's go team up with that group to beat SHINC!* and ambushed them.

When the unwitting teams showed up, no idea that the flares were stolen, they thought *Huh? Where are our comrades?*

When they found only Tanya, their enemy, they would yell "After her! Finish her off!" then engage in a fierce pursuit when she ran away.

"Aaaagh!"

Only to be slaughtered in an instant by the other four members who were lying in wait for Tanya to return.

During the Satellite Scans at 12:20 and 12:30, Boss stood alone in a location a few hundred yards from the rest of the team. The other five members would set up a trap around the location of the flare gun, then ambush the next group of naïve enemies, beating them handily.

Not a single one of the squads that SHINC dispatched ever succeeded in meeting up with any of their comrades in the plan.

Among the defeated squads was one featuring the man from SJ2 who made the most of his experience by providing his own running commentary. The rest of his team died first, leaving only him hanging by a thread with several bullet wounds.

"Shot in the right hand! Now the left! That's my leg! Fell down! Numb from shock! Big bad shot!" he blurted out, like it was freestyle rapping. The sight was so curious that SHINC briefly stopped shooting at him.

When they ripped his Type 89 gun away, his hit points were nearly gone. He lay faceup on the ground; there was nothing left for him to do but die.

"Oh, this is that commentary guy. We all watched your video from the last one for research."

"Are you recording right now, too? I hope that when we see this, it'll be after we've won," said Tohma and Anna, the two beautiful snipers.

"Thanks for the views! Tell everyone to like and subscribe!" he said pleasantly.

Once she had confirmed the others were dead, Tanya walked

up and pointed her Strizh at the man's face. "Sadly, your valiant battle ends here. I'll give you the mercy of a swift end. Do you have any last words?"

"Yes!" he said. To the three women present and the entire audience watching, he shouted words that truly came from his heart.

"Before I die! I would be very happy if, just once, I got to touch some boobs!"

Blam-kaboom-kabam-blam-blam-blam-blam!

The video of several fierce-looking women all blushing as they mercilessly blasted him with their guns eventually went on to rack up considerable views, but that would all come after the end of SJ3.

CHAPTER 9

What MMTM and ZEMAL Were Doing

SECT.9

CHAPTER 9
What MMTM and ZEMAL Were Doing

Memento Mori, abbreviated as MMTM, spawned in the middle of a forest in the northeast corner of the map.

The east and northeast parts of the map were tree-covered flatlands. Many of the trees were deciduous with wide leaves, and the plains featured tall, waist-high grass, so it was a place with little long-term visibility.

At worst, they could only see ten feet in front of their faces, and at best, they could see about a hundred feet away. It was similar to the jungle environment from the last Squad Jam.

While the elevation was essentially flat, the ground itself undulated a fair bit. With the addition of fallen trees and heavy patches of grass and shrub, it was a very difficult environment to run through.

The sky was also almost entirely hidden from view behind all the branches and leaves, making the surroundings very dark. There'd be a picture of this forest in the dictionary under the word *gloomy*.

It was brighter to the north and to the east, but they quickly learned that was because the trees ended in ocean there. And not only that, the water level was rising.

"Aha, so that's what they're doing to us," said MMTM's team leader, grinning to himself. He gazed out at the approaching sea. "Sounds fun! All right, boys, let's make use of this!"

*   *   *

12:10.

MMTM hadn't appeared on the monitors at all, because they hadn't been in battle. The audience in the pub had no idea what was happening with them yet.

When the first Satellite Scan arrived, the results were displayed on-screen for them to follow, too.

"So MMTM's in the upper right," they said, confirming that the four strongest squads were in the four corners of the map. "So what are they going to do first?" they wondered, anticipation running high.

On the map, they saw MMTM in the northeast corner, with a number of other teams scattered around them at distances of at least two-thirds of a mile apart.

At that moment, the screen switched to another team. They were in a dark forest, so it had to be one of the teams close to MMTM. Six men huddled deep in thick grass, watching their surroundings warily.

They all wore camo patterns of black and dark gray. They also had black beanies and goggles that hid their eyes, plus masks featuring gray skulls.

They wore military headsets with mic arm attachments. These were useful tools for talking to remote team members in the real world, but since *GGO* already featured tiny communication items as small as hearing aids, these were probably more for effect than any practical purpose.

Every last member of the team carried an HK416D 5.56 mm assault rifle.

The HK416 series was essentially Heckler & Koch's line of M16 rifles, and they were excellent examples within that category, some of the most expensive that players could find in *GGO*. There were barrel options of various lengths; this group had chosen the shorter ten-inch variety for greater mobility.

Not only were all six decked out in the same gear, they even coincidentally had avatars of similar builds—average heights and average weights. It was impossible to tell any of them apart. Unlike T-S, they didn't feature numbers on their uniforms. It was like looking at sextuplets. It would've been very considerate of them to distinguish themselves with individual color themes. This was all intentional, of course. Making themselves look identical served a tactical purpose of deceiving the enemy. Then again, when they were *this* similar, they'd have to worry that they might not actually be able to tell one another apart, either.

One of the men put his device back in his pocket at the end of the scan, pulled a signal flare from his vest pocket, checked the color, then shot it.

The shining blue light rose upward—and then it fell back down.

Huh?

The man's skull mask hid his expression, but anyone could easily imagine him wondering that, as the blue flare fizzled on the ground near the group of six.

"Uh, what were those guys trying to do exactly?"

"Beats me," muttered the audience in the bar.

The team was aware of the plan to shoot up flares, like all the others were doing, but the canopy of the forest prevented them from actually sending up the signals. And even if it somehow got through, no one would be able to see it from the ground under all the trees.

The audience in the pub wouldn't figure that out until a little later, but for the skull-mask team out in the wild, it was an extremely pressing problem. A huge one, in fact.

"Dammit! They're useless to us now!"

The name of their squadron was Hohoemi Tayasars. It was kind of a cheeky way of saying "Never-ending Smilers," in the way that some old-fashioned Japanese folk singers might have named their band. Whoever came up with the name, it seemed intended to clash with their visual aesthetic, what with all the drab colors and menacing skulls.

It was clear they were making the most of their time in *GGO*, however. Their abbreviated tag was HTS, and this was their first Squad Jam.

They were survival gamers.

Their type of game was the offline sort that used low-pressure gas or air-powered guns that did not violate Japan's strict laws against weapons. When shot, it was on the victims to uphold the honor code and announce their casualties.

This sport started in America as paintball and evolved into airsoft gun battles in Japan. It was a popular sport all over the world, and as of 2026, airsoft guns were manufactured everywhere. It was very common for a proper gun maker to announce a new model, then produce airsoft versions of it to sell as additional products.

Because learning to handle a gun was much safer when it was airsoft, and they made for good close-combat training, militaries around the world began to use them in official training exercises.

So did the arrival of full-dive virtual reality games like *Gun Gale Online* completely wipe out the survival-game industry? The answer was no.

For one thing, many people were afraid of full-dive VR. There was no denying that the biggest contributor to that was the *Sword Art Online* Incident, in which nearly four thousand people lost their lives.

And even in the absence of any fear or distaste for full-dive VR, plenty of people still preferred to use their own bodies and muscles for the pleasure of engaging in simulated battle with airsoft guns.

It wasn't an issue of one being better than the other. Plenty of gun fanatics enjoyed both equally. Some people started with survival games and migrated to *GGO*, and others got into the VRMMO first before trying out survival games.

The members of HTS were the sort who got into both real

and virtual battles. They got their start in survival games, however—they'd been at it for over a decade. It was five months ago that they started playing *GGO* together. They hadn't been playing for very long, but they had a rich history of personal experience to back them up, and they used their well-oiled teamwork to hunt monsters, fight the occasional battle against other players, and power up their characters.

In the deep darkness of the forest, HTS spoke with muffled voices through their skull masks.

"What should we do? MMTM is close."

"I don't know if we have a choice... The flares are useless here."

When the first scan arrived moments ago, they saw that MMTM was just over half a mile to the east, right at the border between forest and sea.

Not only that, HTS was easily the closest team to them. There were four others within a two-mile range.

If they could use the signal flare properly, their comrades would come to join them, and they only had to wait and defend themselves against a charge from MMTM.

"Ah, back to the drawing board! Forget the flare strategy!"

"All right. So much for that."

"What should we do, then?"

"That's easy!"

Five of them were looking at the sixth, who had to be the team leader, but as soon as they started moving, it would be impossible to identify him again. He said, "I didn't like that pessimistic plan anyway! Let's take this opportunity to bring the fight straight to them first!"

It was a bit of a Hail Mary strategy, but his teammates welcomed it.

"Hell yeah! Let's do it!"

"Couldn't ask for a better challenge!"

"Even if we lose, we'll be famous if we manage to put the hurt on the heavyweight contenders!"

"I'm in! Let's do it big, boys!"

"No objections here!"

The six survival gamers turned *GGO* players rushed through the woods. Visibility was poor, the undergrowth was thick, and the ground was loose under their feet.

Team HTS worked with all the leg power they had, but it still took them about five minutes to travel half a mile, including a number of spills along the way.

It was the kind of movement that was likely to transition into a sudden battle, so their charge was captured on camera for the audience the entire time.

The team of six proceeded through the forest, each member about five yards apart, HK416D in his hands, making an arrow formation. The point man was at the tip, with two men on his right, two on his left, and one more in the rear.

The audience had picked up on the problem with the flares at this point, so they reappraised the squad's actions.

"I see. Guess they're gonna try tackling MMTM head-to-head, then."

"So they'll just rush 'em and start an all-out battle? I got no problem with a mad charge that might go down in flames."

"Yeah. And if luck's on their side, and they take out even one member of MMTM, that deserves a medal."

The audience was made up of fellow players of *GGO*, so they understood the rationale behind their strategy. It was going to be an all-out attack on MMTM. Since visibility was poor in the forest, they might even get into a close-range gunfight. Even better if it turned into a melee.

So how would the fearsome MMTM respond? The audience waited for the answer by holding their collective breath—or, alternatively, swigging from their drinks.

Bchonk.

The battle began with an explosion.

The point man for HTS died in a single shot. He was running at full speed when an explosion occurred right before his eyes, and he blew into digital smithereens. He'd noticed something just before it happened and was in the process of moving the muzzle of his gun, but was not in time to do anything about it.

"A hundred feet! Grenadier!" shouted one of the men on the right wing of the arrowhead formation as he began firing. It was on semiauto, shooting one round with each pull of the trigger, but his interval was short and quick.

He saw the man who shot his teammate. It was a man in Swedish military camo hiding behind a thick tree farther away in the forest. He'd watched the video of the last time around, so he recognized the MMTM outfit and the weapon.

It was the handsome avatar of MMTM's leader, who used the Austrian Steyr STM-556 assault rifle. Below the gun barrel, it had a single-shot grenade launcher attached.

His teammate had been unlucky to take a direct, fatal blow from a grenade, but it did tell him where the man was—very close. Given how much the tree trunks blocked their view, he probably couldn't have gotten a shot until now.

As for the other members of MMTM, their locations were still unknown. But that didn't stop HTS.

"I'm fine with one for now! Get him!"

"Yeah!"

They continued their forward movement, popping off shots as they went. Firing as they moved was an effective way of putting pressure on the enemy. Whether he reloaded his launcher or started shooting with the rifle, not many people could stay calm with so many bullet lines converging on their location.

Playing survival games had taught them that, whether in boxing or in gunfights, throwing more attacks than the other side enabled attackers to push them around.

"Push, push, push!"

The five men approached the place where they saw MMTM's leader.

"Oh! Do you think...this is actually working?" one of the audience members asked hopefully.

The very next moment, a green mass swayed and rose on the screen, then smashed into the men in skull masks from behind.

It looked as though the forest itself was attacking them. Like the overgrown grass on the forest floor had just bitten human prey.

As a matter of fact, that was wrong.

The mass of green was people—people wearing ghillie suits that took camouflage one step past patterns and used detailed strips and twigs colored green to heighten the effect.

On top of that, the men had cut down all the grass in that area, then arranged it on their outfits to make it look like it was growing on them instead. The end result was a group of puffy green men who were indistinguishable from the forest background, even at extremely close range.

They kept their faces clear of grass for visibility, but a bit of green face paint went a long way in adding to the disguise.

"Gaagh!"

The men were completely taken aback by the blow from behind. They toppled forward or sideways, depending on the angle they were hit.

Then the mass of green folded in on the group of fallen men, who had lost the timing of their shooting.

Glint!

Dark blades flashed in the disguised men's hands, mercilessly slashing at their victims' throats and chests.

"Gweh!"

"Hurgh!"

"Aaah!"

One by one, they suffered huge HP losses and perished.

"Huh? Huh?"

The one man who was lucky enough not to be attacked panicked in the midst of the suddenly silent forest. His HK416D waved back and forth in search of a target.

Pshoom!

A single, perfectly placed bullet hit him right in the forehead, killing him instantly.

About twenty yards away, MMTM's leader lowered his STM-556 and gave an order to his squadmates.

"Finish him."

The last surviving member of HTS finally recognized the green mass that enveloped him as being an enemy—and then as a human being.

"Huh? W-wait, time out, wait—," he tried to protest.

"..."

But the man with bright-green face paint merely lowered the combat knife onto his hapless victim's goggles. The tip split the lens easily, then the eye of the avatar, and lodged straight into his brain.

The one thing no one would ever see in a survival game was direct hand-to-hand attacks.

"Hey—no—wait—that's messed up!"

There's no way I can defend against this, the man thought ruefully as he was knocked out of SJ3.

Twenty seconds later, MMTM's leader issued a command to his team as he checked the area with his STM-556 at the ready.

"Sitrep."

One by one, his five comrades reported that they had eliminated their targets.

"Good. We'll do this again for the next one," he said.

*   *   *

They set their leader apart as a decoy during the satellite period. If they waited in a place closer to the sea, they wouldn't need to worry about an attack from behind. And when the enemy team came to attack, five perfectly disguised ghillie suit warriors would lie in wait, blending in with the forest as their prey unwittingly walked right past them.

Then, when they judged the moment was right, they would strike at close range. Rather than guns, they used direct physical blows and combat knives to minimize the sound.

MMTM used this spiderlike trap strategy to eliminate team after team. While SHINC loudly and violently drew attention to themselves with flares and gunfights, MMTM survived with stealth and silence.

After the 12:20 scan and the 12:30 scan, more bodies joined the forest floor.

Each team entered the woods without meeting up with their coconspirators—and none of them ever left it. It was like some cursed forest in an old fairy tale.

No one fired their guns aside from the squad leader, and MMTM quickly racked up the kills.

"These guys still freak me out," someone in the audience murmured.

*   *   *

Slightly earlier at 12:18, there was one team raising one hell of a clamor in the center of the city on the northern side of the map.

Blam-blam-blam-blam-blam-blam-blam-blam-blam-blam!

"Whoooooooooooooooooooooooooooo!"

The gunfire was merciless—and the screaming just as overbearing.

By this point, it should already be obvious which team this was. That's right, it was the All-Japan Machine-Gun Lovers, who went by the tag ZEMAL. The team that suffered a hail of bullets from

Llenn in SJ1 and who vastly improved their performance in SJ2
until they got killed from atop the walls.

Five manly men, each equipped with a manly machine gun.

On this day, ZEMAL did what they did best: let loose with
their guns.

Right in the middle of the street, in fact.

"What the hell is that?!" yelled one of the audience members,
and he couldn't be blamed.

Nobody could have predicted what was on the screen now.

If it could be described in a short series of words, it would be:
shopping cart machine-gun turret.

It was an extra-large shopping cart as often seen in the United
States, the kind big enough to fit a small sofa inside or seat a
full-grown adult. The frame was silver with rusted spots all over.

On top, near the handlebar and the child seat, was fixed
an M240B 7.62 mm machine gun. This was a massive gun,
twenty-five pounds and nearly four feet long, and it was held
firmly in place with wire.

The ammo belt that hung from the left side of the gun ran down
into the cart, where a backpack was resting. There were hundreds
of bullets in the belt within the pack, so they could keep firing
and firing without needing to feed a new ammo belt in.

Even stranger were the bundles of pipe standing on the edges
of the cart. They looked like plumbing pipes, an inch or so wide,
bundled up ten in one, and then lined up around the outside of the
cart. It looked like a makeshift organ.

That made it a moving turret, with the cart as a base with
wheels and the pipes as shielding around the gun itself.

Blam-blam-blam-blam! Blam-blam-blam-blam-blam-blam!

The ZEMAL man was blasting away in an American-style
neighborhood. On the other side of the two-lane street was an
enemy squad in hiding.

ZEMAL's opponents wouldn't dare show their faces while the

team was firing. A single one of those shots would mean instant death if it struck their heads, whether aimed or by sheer luck.

The cart shook with each shot the gun made, so the bullets were spraying wildly, but that simply made the chance of a lucky coincidental shot landing even higher. It was as scary as could be.

Despite that, one brave man poked his face and gun around a building, keeping low with his left side pressed to the wall. He was dressed in civilian style: jeans, T-shirt, and leather jacket.

He took three quick shots with his AK-47 at the cart, which was just a hundred yards away.

Clang-clang-clang. The bullets hit the bundles of metal piping and were deflected away.

Then the end of the cart and the machine-gun muzzle within it pointed in the direction of the shots.

"Oh, shit!"

A huge bundle of bullet lines appeared, and the man in the leather jacket had to scramble backward. Instantly, the piece of concrete he'd been pressed against a moment earlier was torn to shreds by a hail of bullets. The firing wouldn't stop, so there was no way he could peek out again.

"Screw this! Gotta pull back and find a way to hit them from behind," he commanded to his teammates.

The six of them were hiding out behind a smaller four-story multi-residential building. If they could get into the building and attack from above, that would be great, but unfortunately, all the structures around here were half collapsed, with the roofs fallen in, and they couldn't get inside.

"Got it! Let's rush back a block and swing around them. They can't catch up to us, even with their wheels."

"Okay!"

The men sprinted. They headed away from the main road where the machine-gun cart was firing wildly and ran down the street running parallel to it. After fifty yards, they passed around the side of a building toward a street corner. They didn't want to

jump out headfirst, so they slowed down as they approached the corner for an initial peek.

"There they aaaaare!"

"Gotchaaaaa!"

At that very moment, two more carts came rattling around that corner—along with the machine guns inside them.

It was a very unlucky encounter at a distance of less than thirty feet.

Blam-blam-blam-blam-blam-blam-blam-blam-blam!

Victory smiled upon the side with more firepower.

That was the power of the machine gun, even if it was only two against six.

The M60E3 and FN MAG lit up the unfortunate squadron with a storm of 7.62 mm bullets.

They tried their best to fight back, of course. They'd been taken by surprise, so they let loose with their guns.

But their shots all bounced off the metal pipe barriers erected around the carts.

The machine guns continued to lambast them with lead until all six were thoroughly dead.

The All-Japan Machine-Gun Lovers were in the middle of town when Squad Jam 3 began, in the center of the northern side of the map, about two-thirds of a mile south of the water.

Around them were cracked concrete roads, dilapidated buildings, overturned vehicles, tilted power-line poles, and dull-gray sky.

"Ooh, it's an urban battlefield this time!" the tallest of the five men exclaimed into the stiff breeze. His machine gun was an M240B, a model used by the American military.

His name was Huey. He was a friendly-looking fellow with his brown hair slicked back except for a protruding peak in his forehead like a rooster's coxcomb. Huey was a burly, macho man, if not quite to the extent that M was.

He wore a black pair of combat pants, a T-shirt, and a green fleece jacket. Rather than a vest adorned with pouches, he carried a large backpack.

This time, the whole team wore matching attire. Since they were sticking around, and people were starting to know their name, they decided that maybe it was worth settling on a look, and they made the wise decision to "spend money on something other than machine guns for once."

So the other man who gleefully noted "Strong wind! Good for machine guns!" was wearing the same thing. Down to the same backpack.

His name was Peter. He was the shortest of the five, with a wide forehead and short, scruffy black hair. The tape he put over the bridge of his nose was his trademark feature. For his weapon, he used an Israeli Negev, a 5.56 mm machine gun.

"Hear us, god of machine guns!" prayed a man with a bandana wrapped all the way around his head. He, too, had a powerful, chiseled body.

He used an FN MAG, and his name was Tomtom. He wanted to go by Tom and nothing more, but there were so many Toms in the world that he chose to double it instead.

"The wind is blowing! Right at us!"

"Uh, isn't that the bad way? We want it at our backs, right?"

Those were the last two members of the team.

The one who mistook the direction of the wind played a muscled black avatar, of which there were many in *GGO*, with a very finely shaped fade cut. His name was Max, and he used a Minimi, the most famous of 5.56 mm machine guns. There were many models of Minimi; he used the Mk2 type. It was recognized by its longer fixed stock.

The last member, who had corrected Max, had black hair down to his collar and a sweatband tied around his forehead. His machine gun was the 7.62 mm M60E3. His name was Shinohara, because he didn't feel like coming up with a creative name for his character and went with his own family name. He had no relation to Miyu Shinohara, of course.

When ZEMAL spawned on the SJ3 in their fresh matching duds, their first action was to examine the area. Then they looked at the map, and understood that the entire map, including the city they were in, was an island.

From there, they considered how they would fight.

Technically, the leader of the squad was Huey, the M240B user. But that was only a designation they had to make to participate in Squad Jam. In truth, they all got along well and weren't sticklers about hierarchy.

In SJ2, they found a nice hilly area with good views where they could hide out, and they put together a pretty nice run, all things considered. They came up with some good ideas—finding another good vantage point, perhaps on top of a building, or moving out of the city, where battle range was often short and full of dead ends and blind spots.

"Say, are there any vehicles around here?" Shinohara wondered, and off they went in search.

If there was a car around, they could all pile in and shoot in all directions while moving quickly across the map. That was a very effective strategy for the paved city area.

But after five minutes, they found nothing. All the cars in the urban area were wasted away and ruined.

In the process, Tomtom, the bandana-wearing one, pointed out a building along the road they were walking down. "Maybe there aren't any cars, but doesn't that place look like it would have *something* useful?"

The whole city was run down and ruined, but one of the buildings here was relatively well-preserved. It was a large, long building with a big parking lot. Clearly, it was a retail business of some kind, but the signs were all wasted away, so there was no way to tell what they once sold.

"Yep. It behooves us to enter."

"Let's do it."

They walked into the building, machine guns first.

"Greetings! We are the All-Japan Machine-Gun Lovers!"

It turned out to be a home improvement store, where people could buy all kinds of tools and supplies for DIY projects.

It was on a much larger scale than the stores in Japan, so there really was everything there. If one had the spirit and the expertise, they could probably build an entire house with materials purchased just from this one business.

The roof had fallen in various spots, so the interior was bright. Naturally, all the wood material had rotted away, and the electric tools were entirely rusted and broken. However…

"Hey, think we can use this?" Max, the avatar with dark skin, wondered aloud. He had found a shopping cart with working wheels.

Bing!

Their eyes glinted with inspiration.

There were quite a few working carts, as it turned out. Plenty were crushed or disfigured, but there were so many to begin with that it didn't take long at all to acquire five that would get the job done.

There was plenty of metal wire, too. And pliers. And duct tape. And metal pipes. And a pipe cutter, although it was rusty.

Then it was crafting time.

They propped a machine gun in each cart, making sure it was comfortably balanced, then tied it down firmly with wire. They cut the pipes to just the right length to bundle up with duct tape to make shields, then attached them around the outside of the carts, and…

"Wa-ha-ha-ha-ha-ha! This is awesome!"

They had five fully armed and operational shopping carts blazing through the city.

The connected ammo belts meant they could keep firing, and the metal pipe shields easily deflected enemy bullets. With the wheels, they were highly mobile, too.

They were practically technicals (improvised vehicles with a gun on top, like pickup trucks), except they were powered with good old feet rather than an engine.

With a little bit of ingenuity, ZEMAL had remade themselves into a much stronger force—and they raised hell accordingly. Every team they encountered in the city, they defeated.

Some teams even tried shooting flares to get them on their side instead, but sadly, the man in the red beret hadn't gotten around to telling ZEMAL the big plan.

"What's with that flare?"

"No idea. Shoot 'em."

They came across Team NSS, a bunch of history-loving reenactors who role-played *GGO* as though they were soldiers from the past reincarnated into its future settings. As they went down, each of them cursed their opponents in ways that matched their backgrounds.

"Damn! No one alive in my time ever fought the way they do!"

"What a coincidence; I could say the same! Commie Soviets—what have they built?!"

"It's a new Nazi tank! I must get word of this back to London..."

"I think it's a new American weapon! If only we had a tool like that!"

Before the special rule went into effect, the last person ZEMAL finished off was KKHC's leader. He was hiding in a large dumpster on the outskirts of the city, but the 12:40 Satellite Scan exposed his location.

"Wait up, wait up, here we come!"

He wound up being chased around by five gun-toting shopping

carts until he was shot and killed. It wasn't the kind of thing anyone experienced very often, in real life *or* in *GGO.*

It was in this state that SHINC, MMTM, and ZEMAL reached the announcement and activation of the special rule at 12:52 with all their members still alive.

CHAPTER 10
Betrayers' Choice

SECT.10

CHAPTER 10
Betrayers' Choice

Special rule announcement and activation.

At the end of this message, one person will be designated from each surviving team.

The designation will be spelled out on the terminal of the chosen player.

The designation is not random but chosen for the purposes of game balance by the staff and sponsor observing the event.

Victory conditions will be altered for the chosen players.

The chosen players will leave their teams as betrayers. The betrayers will form a new team that will fight together from this point onward.

For a period of time, all weapons will be locked. Transportation will be provided to send the betrayers to the rest of their team, opening up travel to the UNKNOWN area.

Now go forth and kill. Your former comrades are now your enemies.

12:52 PM.

Every surviving player read the messages that traveled across their Satellite Scanners.

Those who were chosen to be betrayers received their notice.

*   *   *

SHINC's Boss saw the message on her Satellite Scan terminal that said *Congratulations. You are a betrayer.* and gave her honest opinion on the news.

"…Goddammit!"

She showed the screen to her teammates.

"Aaagh! Not Boss!" wailed silver-haired Tanya, cradling her head with her arms.

"No way…" "This sucks…" "Aww…" "Hmm…"

Tohma, Anna, Sophie, and Rosa added groans of distaste.

Sophie the dwarf was especially angry. She was the second-in-command of the team, played by Kana Fujisawa, vice-captain of the gymnastics team.

"What a stupid rule! We should ignore it! Who thought of such a thing?!" she ranted. Her avatar's face was twisted with fury, a sign of her genuine anger. As it turned out, it was the novelist, the sponsor of the event, who thought of such a thing. "I want to kill him!"

She was scary. But Boss was as implacable as a mountain.

"This is a game. And the rules are the rules," she said coolly. "I don't like it, of course. However, shortcuts might be one thing, but obvious cheating is not what I want to do. If I cheat at this rule, the entire audience will know, and they'll talk about it forever."

"…"

Sophie knew how honest and upright Boss was. She fell silent, and her expression softened.

"Well, hey! We'd be mad no matter who got chosen!"

"Yes, Tanya's right. If anything, it's a stroke of good fortune that I was chosen. Now I'll be fighting against you all, but let's just enjoy the experience!"

"Whoo-hoo! You're the coolest, Boss!" chirped Tanya, who was desperately trying to lighten the mood.

"But," interjected the golden-haired Anna quietly, "Boss really wanted to fight against Karen—I mean, Llenn…"

"That's true, but I can still do that on the team of betrayers. Assuming she didn't get chosen, too."

"Well, I suppose you're right..."

"Don't whine about it! Hold your head high! I always wanted to fight against you guys! So try your best to beat me! I'm going to give you everything I've got!" Boss chided the other five. It sharpened their resolve.

Then the sound of buzzing insect wings filled the wasteland. It was coming from the sky—and getting louder—until her ride descended right into the midst of the six.

Naturally, the flying device showed up on the footage being shown in the pub.

"Whoa! A flying platform!" shrieked the mecha-loving members of the crowd.

It was a very odd-looking device, with a circular body about six feet across and several inches thick, four pipe legs for landing, and handholds around the center with room for one person to stand.

Its principle of flight was the same as a helicopter's.

There were two gasoline engines inside the disc body, as well as two propellers that rotated in opposite directions. The engines powered the propellers, providing a powerful downward gust that lifted the body. By turning in opposite directions, the propellers counteracted the torque effect to keep it stabilized.

And that was what made it a flying platform. The format was originally developed and tested by the American military in the 1950s. They got it into a flyable state but could not deliver enough horsepower for it to be practical, so it quietly vanished into the annals of history.

But there was always a demand for a device that would allow an individual the act of easy flight, so with drone technology on the rise, some people said they might return to the concept soon.

The flying platform might not have worked out in real life,

but thankfully, *GGO* was set in a virtual science-fiction world. The platform here flew like a dream, and the audience watched as the betrayer from each team stepped onto the devices and lifted up off the ground.

"What a ridiculous rule! And it's *me*?!"

In the overgrown forest, MMTM's leader's camo-painted face broke as his expression widened so much that the whites of his eyes were extremely visible. He showed his teammates the indicator that he had been chosen.

"Yikes." "…" "Shit." "No way." "Ahhh."

Naturally, the five others in their bumpy, amorphous disguises reacted with surprise and disappointment.

After the whites of his eyes grew, the leader showed the white of his teeth, gnashing them so hard they seemed fit to crack. His shoulders trembled, not from cold, but from anger.

They'd put in all this work to win the event as a team, and now after coming this far, they were going to be split up to fight against one another. It was the most despicable rule one could imagine.

"Screw this!" he shouted, tossing his terminal aside and reaching for the pistol in the holster at his right side. Like his rifle, the M9-A1 was a Steyr. He pointed the 9 mm automatic pistol at his own temple.

"Whoa! Hang on!" shouted Summon, the biggest of the six, holding his arm back. He dropped his SCAR-L assault rifle in the process. The gun fell into the forest undergrowth.

"Don't try to stop me! Let me die!" the man shouted, resisting.

"We are in the palace, Team Leader! We are in the palace!" Summon cried, using his size advantage to pry the pistol out of the suicidal man's hand.

"That's right, Leader! You don't have to die! And what's that 'palace' stuff about, Summon?" wondered Kenta. He was small, with short black hair, and used a G36K rifle. He turned toward the team leader, face covered in camo paint, and tried to console him by saying, "I get that you're angry about the stupid rule, but if you give up, the battle's already lost."

"That's right," said Jake, the skinnier machine gunner with the HK21. "You've got to enjoy it to the end, even if the situation changes! Besides, they said all the weapon functions would be locked, so you can't shoot yourself, anyway."

"I always wanted to get into a gunfight with you!" added Lux, the man in sunglasses with the MSG90.

"Wouldn't it be dope if we faced off against the team leader and still got the W?" said Bold, the ARX160 gunner with the black dreadlocks. They all had bright smiles and easy affectations.

"..."

The man who couldn't kill himself had no choice but to be their enemy.

"All right... I won't be a fool; I promise," he said, prompting Summon to let go of his arm. He put the M9-A1 back in his holster. When he closed his eyes, the expression was very hard to read on his camo-painted face.

Nearby, a flying platform descended, nimbly avoiding branches and spraying the grass underfoot out in a spectacular display.

"..."

The team leader stepped on the odd contraption without a word, grenade-launcher STM-556 over his back, and the engine whined higher as it ascended again.

As it took him up carefully through the branches and leaves, his teammates shrank down smaller and smaller. Even as they blended into the green of the forest, he could clearly see their smiles.

"Whoo-hoo, a team of betrayers!" cheered Huey, leader of ZEMAL, as he looked at his Satellite Scanner. Arranged around him were his four teammates and their five armed shopping carts.

"Wait, so one of our team's gonna be an enemy now? Dang, that sounds fun!" grinned Peter, the one with the tape over his nose.

"Yeah. It means we get the most beautiful gunfight you could imagine: machine gun versus machine gun!" added Max, the one with the fade.

"Whoo! I'm fired up! I'm burnin'!" roared Shinohara, the one with the M60E3.

"I just wanna fight! So who's the traitor, huh? C'mon, raise your hand! Teacher won't be mad," said Huey.

"Oh…it's me," said Tomtom, the one in the bandana. "Look! Do you see these hallowed words?!" He proudly showed off his terminal's screen to everyone.

"Damn, you lucky bastard!"

"I didn't get it!"

"No fair!"

"I'm so jealous! Switch with me!" his teammates lamented. They were all envious.

"No way! I'm gonna get to kick ass!"

"Please, we can make it work! If we trade terminals, it should be fine, right? Gimme!"

"No, trade with me!"

"Hell no! I'm first!"

Tomtom pushed back against his teammates, who seemed likely to attempt ripping the device from his hands soon. Suddenly, there was the dull sound of approaching propellers.

"Oh! Is that the flying object?"

They glanced upward and caught sight of the flying platform descending toward them. It bore down and landed gently atop the street's cracked concrete.

"Here we go. You guys ready to get your asses kicked?" Tomtom taunted. He used the cutter they brought with them from the hardware store to snip the wires holding his FN MAG inside the shopping cart.

Next, he lifted up the backpack stuffed with ammo from the cart, slung it over his shoulder, lifted the gunsling over his other shoulder, and hopped onto the flying platform.

"See ya! Let's meet again on the battlefield!" he said as nonchalantly as if he were going to the corner store. As the machine rose up into the air, they smiled and waved back.

"I'm gonna pump you fulla lead!"

"Hang in there until we can get to you!"

"Be safe! Don't die right away!"

"I'm tempted to shoot you down right now, but I'll resist the urge!"

On top of a building...

"What? A team of betrayers? What is this...?"

A team of six, completely hidden behind body armor and helmets without an inch of skin showing, grumbled at their Satellite Scanners. This was Team T-S, of course.

They stood where a town had once been. With the rapid sea level rise, over half of the twenty-five-story building was now submerged. No other buildings were still above the water level now. The thick mist hid the distant terrain from view, so they were essentially marooned.

The six sci-fi soldiers sat around atop the faded tile roof, some cross-legged, others with legs splayed out.

"This sucks. A special rule that rips apart a team that's been fighting side by side for all this time? That sucks."

Each member had an ID number from 001 to 006 somewhere on his outfit, such as on the back of the helmet or on the shields they wore on their nondominant arms. The man who said that was 005.

"Oh, I'm the betrayer...," murmured 002 sadly. The gun resting on his lap had the outline of a flattened fish. It was a Heckler & Koch XM8 assault rifle; the most typical-length model, known as the baseline carbine.

The *X* in the model name meant it was a prototype. There were talks to have the American military officially implement this gun into their armory, but that plan was eventually scrapped.

In *GGO*, it was a fairly popular gun, thanks to its distinctive silhouette and low-recoil precision. It used 5.56 mm ammo, with the same magazine as the G36 rifle.

This time around, he attached a suppressor to the muzzle of his XM8. That was a classic example of a pricey upgrade, but the members of T-S were the defending champions. Pitohui's sponsor prize was quite extravagant, so they made quite a lot of cash selling off items.

This XM8, however, had yet to fire a single shot in SJ3.

"Oh, so it's you," said 001 lifelessly when he saw 002's screen. The listless way he said it seemed to sum up the entire group's attitude: "At this point, I don't care who it is."

Next, the man with number 004, who was a lefty with his shield on his right arm, suddenly sat up straight. "Hey! It said a flying object would be coming, right?"

"Huh? Yeah," said 002, who was already on his feet in preparation to leave.

"Then couldn't we all get on top of it and jump off along the way?"

"Uh…ohhh!" 002 exclaimed.

"That's it!"

"We can do that!"

"Nice idea!" the other members chimed in.

"That's right! There's going to be a helicopter thing coming!" 002 said excitedly. His face was hidden behind his helmet, but it sounded like he was smiling. "So I can give you all a ride to dry land!"

"Whoo-hoo!" "Yes!" "We can still play!" "Bravo!" "All right!"

The group was delighted.

They celebrated like shipwrecked passengers suddenly catching sight of a rescue boat. The situation actually wasn't far off from that, in fact.

They heard the sound of the approaching propellers.

They saw the flying craft coming their way.

"What is that…?"

And then a tiny flying platform that was clearly only capable of supporting one person landed next to them on the roof.

"………"

The six of them fell silent.

"Let's try it anyway!" said 002, unfazed.

He slung his gun over his shoulder and gestured to the others to get up. While they stood and picked up their weapons, 002 approached the machine to examine it.

The platform was a round one not even six feet across. But while only one person could fit inside the railing ring in the middle, it looked like it had enough space for five more if they all stood on the outer rim of the device. The only drawback was that the propellers rotated inside the body, so if your foot slipped, it was possible that they'd grind it right off.

"Okay, gang! Stand on the lip of the platform! Hold tight to the railing so you don't fall off! And I'll get on the middle after you're ready!"

"Got it!"

They did as he said and carefully stood on the edge of the circle, grabbing the railing to steady themselves. Once they were on, 002 stood in the middle.

"Here we go…"

Vmmm! The engine noise rose in pitch, and the propellers whirred into high gear.

"Flyyy!"

It did not fly. The pitch rose even higher.

"Flyyy!"

It did not fly. The engine seemed to be hitting its limit. It was ready to break down.

"Flyyy!"

It still did not fly.

"Huh…?"

The flying platform screamed and whirred, but it did not rise an inch off the ground. After a few seconds, the rotation of the engine slowed, and it went back into an idling state. There was an unspoken understanding that they were over its weight limit.

"Dammit!" 002 screamed, looking up to the heavens in lamentation.

"So much for that…," 001 murmured, hopping off the edge of the flying platform. The engine rose in pitch again, but it did not change altitude.

Next, 003 hopped off and said, "Good luck!" It did not fly.

"If you last all the way to the end, we all win!" said 006 as he got off. It did not fly.

"I know you can do it!" 005 stepped off. It still did not fly.

Lastly, 004 jumped off and said, "So long!"

In the end, only 002 was left standing atop the platform. The next instant, it nimbly lifted off the ground and zoomed upward.

"Guys…guys… I'm sorry! I'm sorry! I'm sorry!" 002 wailed with all his strength.

His face was hidden behind his helmet, but it sounded like he was crying.

"What the hell is that? Screw you!"

"Who thought up this dumbass rule?!"

"It was that incompetent writer! Just because he's the sponsor, he gets to do this?!"

"If his avatar was right here, I would shoot him dead so fast!"

Four angry men railed against fate on a grassy field.

Their team tag was TOMS, and their common feature was that they all played agility builds. Like Llenn and Tanya, they chose to fight by moving fast enough that the enemy couldn't hit them in the first place.

Until last year, the common meta knowledge of *GGO* was that agility reigned supreme, and it was still very useful, but the lowered weight limit from not having more strength gave them a clear weakness in firepower.

The squad's clothing was clearly chosen for mobility. They wore light outdoor boots that only rose to the ankle, form-fitting tights, and shorts that ended above the knee.

On top, they wore tight-fitting long-sleeve shirts under compact combat vests lined with bulletproof armor.

The gear was all a dark, faded-brown color, a shade known as flat, dark earth. It would help them avoid sticking out against a soil setting, inside a forest, and even in the city.

Their lightweight equipment made them look like trail runners used to jogging on hiking paths. Even the ammo magazine pouches on the stomach of their vests were kept to a minimal number of four.

Their style was that if they needed more ammo than that for a single battle, they'd rather disengage with the enemy and pull more out of their virtual inventory space instead.

The player's weight limit included the inventory, so in that sense, it made no difference whether it was in the inventory or on their person—but it did change the physical size and surface area of the player. If they were going to slide through tight spots at high speed, the fewer objects jutting off your person, the better.

It was also important for them to *look* more agile. The power of faith would bring them good fortune in this regard.

Heavy weapons required more strength and lowered speed, so everyone in TOMS used a light, practical gun—meaning submachine guns and more compact assault rifles.

As for a precise accounting of those weapons…

One of them was the Heckler & Koch small SMG, the MP7A1. This gun was designed with the same concept as Llenn's P90: shoot bullets faster and harder than a pistol but from a small gun. While typical submachine guns fired pistol bullets, this one used a smaller caliber that traveled faster.

The other three had compact assault rifles, the sort classified as carbines. One had another Heckler & Koch model, the HK53, another used the Korean K1, and the last had a Russian AKS-74U.

TOMS started SJ3 in a field on the eastern part of the map. It was close to the Unknown region, but they couldn't actually see it. When the signal flares went up after the first Satellite Scan, they had the option of going after LPFM or T-S.

"There's more glory in defeating the defending champions."

"Yep. Agreed."

So with that noble decision made, they headed north toward the town. But with T-S being over the water, they were literally out of reach. TOMS had no choice but to join the group battle instead.

They made the most of their speed in the chaotic urban combat, ultimately surviving to become one of the six remaining teams. But in the course of the battle, they lost two members, and the survivors were injured here and there. They'd used up all their healing kits, and they only had about 60 percent of their combined health left. That meant they'd suffered a lot of damage.

Now, with the new rule, they would be losing another of their members.

"Screw this!"

Of course they were mad.

"So, who's the betrayer, huh?" demanded the man with the K1 slung in front of his body. The MP7A1 man showed the others his screen. "It's me..."

"It had to be Cole... The fastest guy on the team...," one of them lamented.

Cole's avatar was the youngest-looking of the bunch. He was white, with brown hair and gray eyes. He grinned and said, "Not quite! Let's use this to our advantage!"

"What do you mean?"

"I'm joining the team of traitors, but I don't need to try that hard to focus on winning! So I'll make a show of being all-in, and at the most opportune moment, I'll betray *them*!"

"That's...actually a great idea."

"Betraying the team of betrayers! I like it!"

"And nobody would expect it!"

Cole lowered his voice to explain the plan, though it really wasn't necessary. "See, here's how it'll happen. On the other side, I'll just run away and focus on surviving. You guys should do the same. With our speed, we can guarantee survival. We'll get the big teams to beat one up another. I'll look for the right opportunity to shoot my own teammates in the back. They won't be expecting it! And once I take the whole team down, I'll kill myself. That way, TOMS will win!"

"Cole... I gotta say..."

"You're the model image of a teammate..."

"You gotta let me buy you dinner sometime...," the others said, getting sniffly. Suddenly, the flying platform descended from the sky.

"Aha! I guess I just ride on this thing. All right, gang, see ya later!" Cole said with a smile, and he jumped onto the platform, clearing the handrail entirely to land inside it.

That explained how five of the six teams' betrayers were chosen and forced to leave their original teams. Not all were simply upset with it, however—there was excitement and conspiracy involved as well.

As for the last team...

"Whoo-hoo! Yeah! It's meeee! Now I get to fight Llenn!"

In the dip in the field, Pitohui examined the screen of her Satellite Scan terminal with a truly malevolent smile.

"What?" Llenn said in disbelief.

Before her eyes, the woman in the navy body suit was crowing with delight. "Yessss! Yahoooo!" What was she, a child? "I'm! The! Betraaaayer! I'm! The! Betraaaayer! Oh yeah, baby!" she sang on the spot. "Loo-loo-loo, la-la-laaa! Ah, how beautiful it is to live the betrayer's life!"

This was where being Elza Kanzaki, the star singer, really came in handy. She could even make weird improv songs sound good.

"Aww, you're so lucky, Pito. Switch with me! I'm good at flying, you know. I fly every day in *ALO*! Exchange terminals with me!" clamored Fukaziroh, pouting at Pitohui's side.

"Not so fast! This is a very important part of the game set up by the developers. Obey the rules!" Pitohui scolded as she put her device away.

"Huh…?" Llenn still couldn't process what was happening before her eyes.

"It had to be you, of all people… Well, go on and enjoy yourself, I suppose," M said with a grunt.

"As if I need to be told that by you! Why don't you focus on not dying before I get the chance to kill you, M?"

"I'll do my best."

Then Fukaziroh chimed in happily, "Fine, Pito, I'll kill you! Which would you prefer, plasma grenade or pistol?"

"What? You're a terrible shot with the pistol, Fuka."

"I mean that I'll pistol-whip your skull! A hundred blows should do it, right?"

"Ohhh, that sounds painful. I'd become a vegetable from concussions long before that point."

"Ah, that's an option, too."

"But I'll be fine, because you won't get anywhere close to me. If you've got a problem with that, feel free to prove me wrong!"

As Fukaziroh and Pitohui bantered, an odd flying vehicle came buzzing over. It picked out a spot of flat ground about ten yards away from the hollow they were hiding in and landed noisily on the grass.

"Oh! So I get on that for a ride!"

Pitohui picked up her KTR-09 with one hand and skipped happily over to the flying platform.

"…"

Llenn could only watch in silence.

"Hmm, will I actually be able to ride this?" Pitohui wondered, uncharacteristically doubtful. She lifted her foot and stepped into the circle. Instantly, the engine whirred louder, and the platform lifted off the ground.

"Ha-ha! I'm riding it! Yay! Well! Hey, guys! Oh—and Llenn! Hello! Llenn?"

Llenn was dazed. "Ah!" she said, coming to with a start and looking up to where Pitohui was rising into the sky.

"Llenn! I'm going to come looking for you first! So look forward to that! I'm not going to die right off the bat! Make sure you beat me before you beat SHINC! Ah-ha-ha-ha-ha-ha-ha!" she shouted with a loud laugh, combining a dazzling smile with violent threats. The platform took her off into the cloudy sky.

"Ah-ha-ha-ha-ha-ha—"

Eventually, her voice cut out of the comm signal in their ears. Whether she had turned it off herself or it stopped functioning because they were no longer teammates, no one on the ground could say.

Down in the grass, Llenn practically screamed, "*Aaaaaaaa aaaaagh!*"

"Ooh-hoo! We get to fight Pito again! Yippee!" chattered Fukaziroh, whose gamer's soul was thrilled by this development.

Always the calm and measured one, M said, "This is a dangerous foe to deal with... Now we need to think of some strategies for the three of us..."

"Bwa-ha-ha! This is so fun! I'm flying!" Pitohui said, enjoying her virtual flight and bubbling with anticipation about a future duel with Llenn. She had the KTR-09 slung over her back and spread her arms in a flying pose.

The platform was entirely autonomous. It flew all on its own no matter what the rider did or how it tried to affect the balance. Once they were on it, there was nothing to do. Of course, the real-life prototypes in the 1950s could not do any of this, but that was just some good old *GGO* magic.

Once she reached about five hundred yards in height, there were only clouds above, but the view below was excellent. In the distance, the sea and shoreline were visible, so she could tell which way she was going: toward the Unknown area at the center of the island.

Soon there was a little dot that came into view on the right side of the direction she was traveling. It grew larger and larger until she could make out its form—another flying disc with a person on top of it.

"Oh, one of my 'companions,' eh? Maybe I should shoot them down," Pitohui muttered, for some reason, prepping her KTR-09. But when she put her finger on the trigger, no bullet circle appeared; the weapon was still locked.

"Ah well. I'll have plenty of chances to kill them," she said menacingly, lowering her gun.

On the screens in the bar, all six flying platforms were shown in close-up. It was easy to tell who was riding on them, naturally.

SHINC's Boss, with her silenced Vintorez.

MMTM's leader, with an STM-556 with attached grenade launcher.

ZEMAL's bandana man, equipped with an FN MAG machine gun.

T-S's 002, with the prototype XM8 assault rifle.

TOMS's MP7AI shooter, though few people knew much about that team.

"It's that chick!"

And lastly, Pitohui, with the KTR-09 assault rifle, among many other weapons.

"Holy crap, man! That's an amazing party."

"And they're all gonna be one team now...?"

"Do they seem super-tough to you, too? Especially after messing up the balance of the teams who lost members."

"But the devs and the sponsor are the ones watching the match and picking them out, right?"

"You know how messed up that sponsor is. He probably picked them hoping that the betrayers would win, right?"

"I think it would be dope if they were fighting against everyone else together."

"I wanna see that!"

As the crowd raved and buzzed, the six flying platforms made their way toward the center of the island—toward the mysterious place surrounded by impenetrable mist, represented on the map only by a block that read UNKNOWN.

There was an unnatural wind blowing through the world of Squad Jam 3, a gust stronger than any felt previously.

It caused the flying platform carrying ZEMAL's Tomtom to rock, and he grabbed the railing and shrieked, "Aieee!"

It was a strong enough gale that it blew away the unnatural mist in an unnatural fashion. The mist had been blocking any visibility beyond a mile, but now it cleared up at a rate that was simply impossible in real physics. It was like a veil being swept aside.

And before the eyes of the six players on flying platforms—and the crowd watching on the screens—and atop a distant hill for Llenn and the other players left behind on the fields of the island...

...they saw something.

A ship.

It was a ship that was hidden in the Unknown area.

A deluxe cruise ship, right in the middle of the island, resting atop the gentle crest of the hill there.

The ship was tremendous in size: 1,600 feet long, three hundred feet wide, and about three hundred feet tall above the waterline. The bottom part of the ship was embedded in the earth, so it was probably closer to 330 when counting that—and even more with the mast and antenna.

There was a bulbous bow at the bottom of the front end of the ship to minimize water resistance, but it was buried underground at this moment. In fact, the body of the ship was embedded in the soil in perfect balance, maintaining an almost entirely even keel

from side to side and fore to aft. The ground even went right up to the waterline, so it looked as though it was cruising on a sea of green.

The body of the ship was white, but it had faded with age, turning parts of it cream or gray. There were also dirty brown spots and some noticeable vertical red streaks that were probably rust.

On the sides hung countless balconies from all the cabins. By counting the levels of windows and balconies, one could arrive at the conclusion that the ship had twenty decks in all.

"Yowza! It's huge!" Pitohui cheered.

"What an enormous ship," said Boss.

"So they want us to fight on this," murmured MMTM's leader, when he caught sight of the tremendous vessel from above.

"The final stage!"

"Whoa, that's big!"

"Ah! A ship!"

"Oh, I knew that. The middle of an island? Gotta be a ship."

"You were the guy who said earlier 'It can't be anything other than an airship,' right?"

The audience in the pub was also oohing and aahing over the enormous cruise ship. At last, the Unknown area had been revealed. The aerial camera caught the ship at an angle, so they could see its details quite clearly.

There was a wide, flat space at the prow of the ship, with a circle painted green, and in the middle, though faded and missing at parts, was clearly an *H*. This was the helipad.

Behind that was the upper body of the ship, rising like a mountain. Glass windows lined the smooth incline. Since it was a ship, the tallest deck featured the bridge, where it jutted out with curved glass for visibility.

Moving toward the rear of the ship were the stacks of decks, balconies, and windows. Many were broken. Had the ship hit something at some point? Some of the balconies were notably crushed.

"The cabins seem pretty torn up."

"Well, this ship would be from before the big war."

"In that sense, it's remarkably well preserved."

The lower promenade deck on the sides of the ship—where there were no cabins, just walkways—featured a number of lifeboats with bright-yellow tops for visibility. There were many of them, since they were meant to hold all the passengers, which was a considerable amount. The lifeboats were packed end to end all along the sides of the cruise ship. They were like aphids crowded on a leaf, as unsavory as it was to say.

Their paint was also damaged with age, but the boats themselves were all intact and seemed usable.

The cameras switched to an angle directly over the ship, traveling from the prow toward the stern. They passed over a wide space in the middle.

It was built in such a way that the cabins ran along the sides of the ship, while a courtyard of sorts opened up in the middle where the sun could reach. This area was about two-thirds the ship's length, so over a thousand feet long—and a good 160 feet across.

Given the size of the deck space, there were many different features there. It was hard to make out details from the overhead shot, but viewers could see what looked like a park, some foot paths, and some freestanding carts.

On top of the cabin areas on either side were pools and Jacuzzis full of muddy, rancid water. There was even a filthy basketball court, as well as some jutting smokestacks. Some bridges crossed over between the port and starboard sides here and there. Above that was the tallest point on the ship, an observation deck.

The aerial view continued scrolling, and the ship kept going. And going and going.

"That thing is enormous."

"It's like an apartment complex."

"It's bigger than my whole hometown."

A minute or so after it started, the camera finally scrolled to the ship's stern. It was a wide, flat, open space connected to the internal courtyard, with a half-circle stage set slightly lower at the end. It was a large stage with rows of descending benches for an audience to sit upon.

Behind the stage was a wide deck for watching the trail in the water behind the ship. Because there were only waves behind that point, there was a tall and sturdy railing running along it.

It was a gorgeous behemoth of a ship.

The audience could easily imagine it in its glory days, pristine and shining as it kicked up wake behind it.

It probably hosted countless memories, with thousands of passengers—friends, families, lovers—having the time of their lives on its many decks.

Others probably watched the cruise ship from the shore, dreaming of the day that they, too, could travel the world in luxury.

So why was it stuck in the ground in a place like this? The camera switched to the side of the prow, as if offering an answer.

There, written in a graceful English font on the side of the ship, was its name: Conqueror of the Seven Seas. Except that it had a huge X drawn over it. Below that point, a new name had been scrawled. It was sloppy and ugly, clearly painted by hand.

The new name of the ship was *There Is Still Time*.

"Ah, I get it. That's some *GGO* set dressing. Would've happened after the big apocalyptic war."

"Brutal, as always."

The audience members commented one after the other, understanding the environmental storytelling at play.

GGO was set on an Earth in the far future, after humanity engaged in an ultimate war with nuclear weapons—and probably things even worse than that. The environment was destroyed, and even the few humans who survived eventually died out in the generations after the war.

The people on Earth now—the players of *GGO*—were the ones who returned to the empty planet from space on the Space Battle Cruiser *Glocken*.

Among the players of *GGO*, there were more than a few who said, "I can't get enough of this postapocalyptic Earth. Honestly, I'd have fun without shooting a single gun here." They enjoyed taking in the conflicting feelings of familiar man-made settings that were decayed and destroyed. They were like urban explorers who got a kick out of exploring abandoned buildings that nature had reclaimed.

These folks formed squadrons with like-minded individuals who dedicated themselves to exploring the world that had been built for them. They'd go out on expeditions, enjoying the remote locales, and sell the items they found—usually guns or gun designs—for cash to fund the next expedition.

They would carry around guns, too, of course, but not to aggressively attack monsters and other players, merely to defend themselves if needed. They didn't see themselves as soldiers, but as explorers.

In the present day of 2026, there was a good variety of VR games out there, but only *GGO* featured this kind of postapocalyptic setting, especially one set so many years after its downfall.

So the overwhelming scope of its ruination was like ambrosia to the people, whether American or Japanese, who were drawn to that vibe.

And to keep those people interested and live up to their expectations, *GGO*'s environmental designers poured tons of effort into their work, filling them with details. Such as the ruined church with the shining wedding dress inside it that Pitohui once told Llenn about.

This ship, too, had a dark past.

It carried people who somehow survived the apocalyptic war

and sought refuge somewhere else, a brand-new safe land where they could live.

They were the ones who rechristened the *Conquerer of the Seven Seas*, giving it a name full of hope, telling its passengers that there was still time for humanity.

It probably started sailing the seas with thousands, if not tens of thousands, of refugees crammed into its cabins. They must have believed that there was a new paradise awaiting them somewhere.

But something happened, perhaps a tectonic shift or a huge tsunami. The ship went aground atop this mountain and never sailed again.

In fact, perhaps this place *was* the new world they sought.

Whatever happened to those passengers after that point was unclear. The only thing anyone knew for certain was that they were long dead.

"What a gorgeous, sad setting…"

"And now that we've come back from space, we're gonna go and fight it out there!"

"Ah, the tragic nature of man…"

"Let's make a toast and offer a prayer for those who died…and those who are about to die!"

The battle-loving companions raised their glasses toward the ceiling of the pub.

While the audience enjoyed their mock memorial, Pitohui's flying platform was close enough to the ship now that she, too, could read its hull.

"Oh? Ah, that must be her name."

The prow was pointed straight south, so her path toward the ship took her right past the writing.

"*There Is Still Time?* Ah, I get it!" she said as the ship grew larger and larger with proximity. "Pfft! Ha-ha-ha! And after all that pointless effort, they all died anyway! Ah-ha-ha-ha-ha-ha! If you're going to die, at least go out in a blaze of glory against your enemies! Ah-ha-ha-ha-ha-ha-ha!"

She laughed long and loud.

"Guess I'll keep the killing going, then!"

The flying platform descended toward the heliport on the fore of the ship, carrying a woman with the straightforward personality of some god of chaos and disaster. The other five platforms were in view, too, arriving from other directions.

They headed down to the setting of the final battle of third Squad Jam.

CHAPTER 11

There Is Still Time to Battle I

SECT.11

CHAPTER 11
There Is Still Time to Battle I

"No time to be sitting around on our laurels."

It was 12:56.

M seemed to have noticed something after Pitohui left, so he turned to his remaining two squadmates, Llenn and Fukaziroh, and commanded, "Run for the center of the island. Full sprint."

"Huh? Whoaaaaa!" Fukaziroh exclaimed as she, too, realized what had changed.

It was the sea.

The speed of its rise was even faster than before. In fact, the water was already within about fifty yards of them. The field was rapidly being submerged by the waves. It was as though some massive living thing was creeping up on them without a sound.

"C'mon, Llenn! Let's go, Llenn!" she urged.

"..."

Llenn sat there dumbfounded until her friend came over and yanked her arm. "Huh? Oh...yeah. I know," she said, getting to her feet.

"Follow me," M ordered, starting to run. She took off a few yards behind him.

M ran in the lead, Fukaziroh to the right behind him, and Llenn to the left. This formation was designed so that hardy M would be in the front, limiting the damage that might befall the smaller girls if he happened to get shot.

Aww... Everyone's doing their best to make me feel better, Llenn thought, feeling her heart prickle painfully.

It hurt, but now was not the time to be down in the dumps. She had to run and keep from going under the advancing waterline.

And once she boarded the giant ship in the distance, she would see Pitohui.

"Let's hurry! Everyone sprint!"

Without Boss, the rest of SHINC took off running. The sea would be upon them if they stayed in place.

The first command came from Tanya. As she ran, she called out the next team leader. "Since Boss is gone now, the next one is Sophie, right? You're up!"

In SHINC, gym-team captain Boss came first, then Sophie, the vice-captain. Next after that was Rosa, for being a third-year, followed by Anna, Tohma, and Tanya by way of a rock-paper-scissors match.

Sophie plodded along as best she could empty-handed—her PTRD-41 was in virtual item storage now.

"Hang in there!" encouraged Rosa, who wasn't very fast, either, holding her PKM machine gun.

Anna and Tohma were the snipers—and fleet of foot. Every now and then, they stopped to scan the area with their Dragunov rifles. It was hard to imagine that any teams would be in a comfortable (or oblivious) enough position right now to start taking potshots at them, but they were prudent.

Tanya sped in the lead and had to stop now and then before she got too far ahead. "What do we do when we get close to the ship? I'm guessing MMTM will be on our right, and Llenn's team will be on our left. Unless she was chosen to be a traitor," she said to the rest of the squad.

As she ran, Sophie replied, "There's no time for fighting. You're forbidden from combat unless absolutely necessary. If there's a ship, that means we need to get on board, or else we drown. Getting on should be our top priority."

"Good point! I guess the other teams are thinking the same thing!"

"Yeah. But…"

"But?"

Five men with camo-painted faces—the members of MMTM—were on the run, passing through the thick forest and out onto the wide-open fields toward the hill at the center of everything.

The ghillie suits were back in their inventories, and the loose branches and leaves they'd piled on top of themselves shook loose as they ran. Those things weren't going to come in handy where they were going.

Up ahead, they could see the rear port side of the luxury cruise ship. But it was still far off, over a mile away.

The leader tag for MMTM had moved to skinny Jake, the gunner with the HK21.

"Hurry, guys! We gotta get there as soon as possible!"

"I know that! This is tough…"

"It's tiring to run like this. Mentally speaking."

He and the others had figured it out. They realized that if they didn't get on that ship as soon as humanly possible, they were going to lose their lives.

And that everyone already on the ship was going to do their utmost to stop them.

✳   ✳   ✳

Around the time that the original teams began to run for it, the cruise ship *There Is Still Time* got its first passengers in many, many years.

On the monitors in the pub, the crowd got a close-up view of the betrayers' team on their flying platforms descending onto the helipad at the fore of the ship.

The six platforms touched down within a span of only twenty seconds. They stepped off the platforms one at a time, and the engines promptly sputtered and emitted white smoke, sending a clear visual signal that they were no longer meant to be used.

The fact that the smoke was traveling directly upward told the audience something.

"Oh, the wind's completely stopped."

The six players made a circle around the *H* on the pad.

It was on the very tip of the enormous ship, so when the camera zoomed out, the people became very, very small.

"Hey, everyone! My new teammates! How are you doing?" Pitohui cried out, the first to speak. She seemed to be doing very well, indeed; she grinned jovially.

"I realize I'm pretty famous, but we can do a round of introductions! List your weapon and your style of combat, too! I'm Pitohui! I use a KTR-09 and some other stuff! You all saw the SJ2 replay, right? Same thing as what you saw there! No Barrett this time, though! I can do just about anything! Nice to meet you! Let's have some fun out there today! Whoo!" she chattered, like the person taking charge of the floor at a drinking party. "You're next, blockhead!"

"Oh, uh… Hello…"

On her left was member 002 of T-S, the large fellow in full body armor. He bowed his helmeted head to the group. In a strangely reserved tone, he continued, "My name is Ervin. How do you do? This is my weapon, an XM8 with suppressor. No pistol. A few grenades."

"Okay, Ervin! Nice to meet you! Let's be relaxed, no fussiness! You were on the winning team last time, right? Be loud and proud! A win is a win, no matter how you do it!" Pitohui encouraged him, sensing his feelings. Everyone knew that T-S got bashed online for how they won SJ2; they were called cowards and cheaters.

"Oh, thanks… That's really nice of you to say, ma…a'am," said Ervin, who couldn't help but be polite in the end.

"Am I the next to go, then?" asked the bandana man on Ervin's left, raising his hand. "My name's Tomtom. I dig machine guns! I love machine guns! Still got lotsa bullets! You want support, you want attack—I'll shoot the hell out of whatever you want! Nice to meet you all!"

He was the kind of person who always had a smile on. His bright and ditzy vibe remained the same, whatever team he happened to be on.

"Nice—good to hear! Next," prompted Pitohui, who had clearly taken the reins. She pointed to the next member.

The man in light gear with a nice, compact MP7A1 said, "Hi, everyone! I'm Cole. I play an agility build. I'm probably the fastest one here! And that means I can also take the least damage before I die!"

He smiled confidently; he understood that in order for his betrayal to be the most effective and devastating it could be, he had to gain their trust first. This was his best initial opportunity.

"This is my weapon! An MP7A1! If we get into any battles in the cramped quarters of the ship interior, lean on me! I work well as a point man and as an attacker!" The self-promotional way he spoke almost sounded like a young person at a job interview.

"Okay. Shall we move on to the last two?" Pitohui said, her tone heavy with knowing sarcasm.

Ervin, Tomtom, and Cole all looked at the two who hadn't yet introduced themselves. Of course they know who these people were. They were both nearly as deadly as Pitohui.

"I'm Eva. As far as my weapons and fighting style go…I'll just flatter myself and assume you already know," said SHINC's Boss, aka Eva, putting one heavy foot forward. Her thick chest—whether muscle or bust, it wasn't clear—puffed out with pride.

No one bothered to contradict her. Nobody would have taken

part in the third Squad Jam without knowing about the runners-up of SJ1 and fourth-place team of SJ2.

She used the silenced Vintorez sniper rifle over her back and the Strizh automatic pistol in the holster at her waist. Strizh was only a nickname that got attached to the gun during its trial period in Russia. Perhaps its official international name, Strike One, would be more recognized.

As she showed in her one-on-one duel with Llenn at the end of the first Squad Jam, Eva was extremely quick for her size. That was a benefit of Saki's real-life athletic reflexes, of course. Because she put plenty of points into her stamina, she could take plenty of hits.

She might be a fearsome enemy, but that meant she was a relief to have on your side.

"That's it? Well, I don't need more info than that anyway. Hi, Eva. I'm happy we get to be on the same team," Pitohui said with a charming smile.

"Sure," Eva replied, her face a craggy mask.

"Then let's go ahead and introduce our last member: Daveed! In fact, he's been playing *GGO* about as long as I have!" Pitohui continued, her tone freewheeling.

"What?!" yelped none other than the man who was last to introduce himself, MMTM's team leader. His eyes and mouth were gaping in the middle of his camo-painted face. He looked rather silly.

"P-Pitohui… You…remember…"

"Yep, I remember you. We were in a squadron together a long time ago, but I never forget anyone I've met before."

"…Well…thanks."

MMTM's leader, whose real name—character name, at least— was David, pulled himself together and said, "I'm the leader of Memento Mori, David. You can also call me Dave. But do *not* call me Daveed!"

It seemed like he had a sore spot in his past about that.

"I use an STM-556 with a 40 mm launcher. I've got the long

barrel on it, too, so I can snipe to mid-distances. And I've got a 9 mm pistol," he explained to the other four. Of course, they'd seen him in the footage of the last two tournaments, so they knew all that already.

Then David added, "To be honest, this betrayers' team rule infuriates me. I'd like to drop a grenade down the collar of whoever thought of it. But for the sake of my comrades who kindly saw me off, I will promise to fight my hardest to the end."

"I like it! I bet we all feel the same way!" Pitohui chirped.

But Cole had to try his hardest not to betray his inner monologue, which went something like: *Heh-heh, not me! Lucky me, I get to reap the reputation of beating this lineup!*

"All right, then! Let's do it, gang!" Pitohui said, wrapping up the introductions. She continued, "By the way, are we going to get to register as a new team? It's inconvenient if we can't see one another's hit points, and it's not fair if we're the only ones who can't talk on the comms!"

"That's true," Eva agreed. "Once I stepped onto that odd device, mine stopped working with my squadmates."

"Do you think it'll work if we apply and register for a new party?" Tomtom suggested.

"Nice one, Bandana! Hang on then, everyone," said Pitohui, gesturing with her left hand. Though the others couldn't see it, she was manipulating her own command window.

Pitohui typed something into an invisible holo-keyboard for a few moments, then waved her hand sideways. Party invitation sub-windows appeared before the other five.

The message said: *You have been invited to join Team Betrayers. Do you accept?* yes/no

So Pitohui had chosen the literal route. Once everyone had hit yes, a new team had arrived in SJ3. Their squad tag automatically converted to BTRY.

"Awright! It's set up! Whoo! Okay! It's always worth a shot! The SJ3 system is awesome!" Pitohui cheered like a little kid. She even hopped around.

It was such an over-the-top celebration that David grumbled, "Of course it was going to work…"

Next, Pitohui switched on the device in her left ear, turned away, and mumbled, "Can you all hear me? Is my sexy ASMR voice coming in?"

"You bet."

"Loud and clear!"

"Very crisp!"

"Yes."

"No problem," the others said in clockwise order, telling her that her own device was receiving signal.

Eva glanced at the wristwatch on her left arm.

It was 12:59. In moments, it would hit one o'clock, and the sixth Satellite Scan would begin.

"What do you think?" Eva asked.

Pitohui answered, "I bet the scan will happen. Let's watch and hold a planning meeting. But before that, how far away were each of your teams when the rule kicked in? Mine was still well over a mile away."

The other four said about the same. Ervin was the only one who said nothing, but everyone else knew where Team T-S had been stuck, so they kindly did not touch upon it.

"Then we've still got time."

Pitohui pulled her Satellite Scan terminal out of her pouch.

1:00 PM.

As expected, the sixth scan arrived, but the island was now unsurprisingly quite small, maybe a mile and a half to a side.

The scan moved quickly, lighting up the dots on the screen.

On the southwest edge of the little island was LPFM. The name hadn't changed, even though Pitohui was gone.

On the southeast corner, also heading toward the ship, was SHINC. Continuing around counterclockwise, MMTM was in the northeast, ZEMAL was in the north, and TOMS was in the northwest.

Lastly, completely isolated out in the middle of the ocean remained the lonely dot of T-S.

And in the center, atop the ship, was of course their own dot, BTRY.

"Yup, I knew it," Pitohui said, putting the terminal back in her pocket. "I might not need this again for the next one."

Everyone else agreed. The next scan would come ten minutes later, but by then, the ship would be surrounded by the five other teams. Looking wouldn't tell them anything they didn't already know.

"Excuse me, who among us would like to be the leader of this team?" asked Ervin, the sci-fi soldier, who still insisted on being polite.

"Miss Pitohui extended the invitation to the rest of us, so she's in that position by default," noted Cole. While he didn't speak quite as politely, he *did* add *Miss* to Pitohui's name.

"That's fine."

"No problem," agreed David and Eva. If the two other toughest characters didn't complain, no one else was going to.

For his part, Tomtom didn't seem to care who was the leader. It was obvious he was itching to shoot his machine gun, and everything else was secondary.

"So what kind of strategy are you going to cook up for us, Team Leader?" David asked, his tone just a bit chilly.

"I've already got one," Pitohui answered immediately.

At 1:03, Llenn's team finally came within half a mile of the ship. They'd been checking the results of the scan as they ran.

They came to a stop, found a lower spot in the field, and hit the dirt in case of snipers from the ship. It had taken quite a long time to get this far, and the sea was still rushing up on them from behind. Llenn could have gotten here faster alone, but she had no choice but to wait for M.

They also kept an eye out for SHINC straight to the east to be safe. They didn't seem likely to attack at this point in time, though, even if Eva had still been on the team.

"It's huge…," Llenn gasped.

The ship was still half a mile away, but it looked as large as a mountain. It was intimidating.

In fact, if it had been an actual mountain, it wouldn't have felt nearly as large. But a ship was a man-made object, and because it wasn't meant to be sitting atop a hill, the eeriness of the image was only amplified.

It felt like the castle of some wicked demon lord. Llenn started to imagine a demonic Pitohui with a black cape flapping in the wind, laughing evilly, and she let out a sigh. "Haaah…"

"If you sigh, your happiness'll fly right outta your mouth," chided Fukaziroh.

"Yeah… Too late for that. Ugh, I can't even imagine what Pitohui's going to do now…," Llenn muttered, not bothering to turn around to face her friend.

"Well, the entire system just guaranteed that Pito's betraying us," said Fukaziroh with a little shrug.

As he watched the ship through the scope of his M14 EBR, M said, "Fuka. Take out all the remaining plasma grenades you have and load them into one of your launchers."

"Oh? How come?"

"Pito knows where you keep them. She'll shoot at your backpack. The metal grenade launchers will provide a bit more defense against bullets, at least."

"Ah, that makes sense!"

Fukaziroh obediently set to the task, switching out the grenades in her left-hand launcher (Leftania) to the plasma kind. There were five of the powerful grenades left.

Llenn kept herself pressed to the ground and watched the cruise ship through her own monocular. The angle was looking onward at the front of the ship from the starboard side. But when she looked at the cliff-like side up to the bottommost deck, she noticed something was missing.

"Huh…?"

Normally, the entrance to passenger ships was on one of the decks, requiring a boarding bridge affixed to the dock or a staircase-like ramp—but neither was visible here.

"M…there are no stairs or ladders; how are we supposed to get on board? Do they expect us to climb the sheer sides of the ship?"

"That's not possible without a really high Climbing skill and the right tools."

"Exactly."

The sides of the ship were an overhang, meaning the angle actually went backward during the climb. No ordinary person could scale that sort of slope.

"Do you think there's a way up on the other side?"

"Probably not," M said. "But I'm not worried. Once we get closer, there should be an entrance, even if it's on the smaller side. I'm certain of it."

"Oh? How can you be so sure?" asked Fukaziroh, who was done switching her munitions.

"That ship was designed to be a refugee ship after the ultimate war. If it got grounded, then the people on board would need a way to get down. If they didn't have a ramp, then they must have opened a hole big enough for people to get through, down near ground level."

"Ah, I see."

"Ooooh!"

Llenn and Fukaziroh were very impressed with M's reasoning. Of course, they could imagine a past in which they pulled up the ramp to stay safe aboard the ship, instead, but that would make things so much harder for the players on the ground. *GGO* was still a game, so they wouldn't set up something that was simply impossible to tackle.

"But since the idea is that the ship sank deeper into the ground over many years, it could have gotten buried or shrank to a smaller size."

That was indeed a possibility. Llenn set her monocular to maximum zoom and focused on the boundary between the side of the ship and the grass below it.

"Ah! There it is! There are holes, just like you said! On the side…about a hundred feet apart?"

They were there. It was very hard to see, but whether exploded out of the steel hull or burned out with heat, there were definitely holes in the ship that wouldn't have formed naturally.

It was hard to gauge the size without an object for comparison nearby, but they certainly were not large. Surely a single person would be able to fit through them, however.

M said, "Good. Then our next task will be getting from here to there, inside the ship."

"Gotcha, gotcha, gotta-gotta-gotcha," Fukaziroh jabbered. "But that raises the question…"

"Once we get closer to the ship, won't the team on top shoot at us?" Llenn finished.

M glanced backward to confirm that the approaching sea hadn't caught up to them yet. Then he said, "But of course. This island is going to sink. That means we die if we don't get onto that ship. Team Betrayers knows that, too. And that means…"

"That means our first priority should be keeping the teams surrounding us from getting onto the ship! That's our first line of defense. If we hold that, we win," Pitohui lectured. No one raised any protest.

The six had left the helipad and were now trotting down the starboard deck. The hallways weren't in good shape, but it wasn't like there were any giant holes that made progress impossible.

David continued behind them, carrying the launcher-attached STM-556 in his hands. "How exactly will we defend this spot? Even if we shoot right over the sides, only Tomtom can get any decent distance," he pointed out.

He was right. The only gun on this team with 7.62 mm rounds and an effective range as high as eight hundred yards was Tomtom's FN MAG. It could fire automatically and often, so his machine gun was quite valuable to the team—but it was only one gun and obviously inadequate to protect the entire perimeter of the enormous cruise ship.

Of course, they could also split up to each cover an individual range of the perimeter and shoot anyone who approached, albeit with shorter range. But that meant getting shot at in return, of course. Since there were far more invaders than defenders, they'd be ducking down out of the line of fire at times. And when they needed to switch magazines, that would leave a long period of undefended approach time for the other side.

On top of all that, it would be an especially disadvantageous position for Cole, whose gun was light and compact at the cost of an effective range of barely two hundred yards.

"It's just too big," Eva muttered, cursing the tremendous size of the craft.

"So here's what I say!" Pitohui decided as she ran in the lead. "First, we need to limit the number of approaches the enemy can take, to limit the amount of space we need to defend. Did you see the holes right near ground level?"

"Yeah," said both Eva and David. They'd been paying close attention while on the flying platforms, and they figured out that those holes were the only entrances for the approaching squads.

The other three were following in silence, not taking part in the planning. They were probably too busy feeling relieved that there were three extremely capable people on the team to do the thinking.

"There were many holes," said David. "We don't have time to trap them all."

To go down belowdecks to the bottom of the ship and place grenade traps around all the many holes in the sides would take way more time and resources than the six of them splitting up could accomplish.

"That'd be impossible. And you won't see any traps until you're

up close on them, right? I want to eliminate the ways in, but specifically, I want to control the approach, to lock down the area
around the ship. And to do that, we need good visibility."

"I understand your point, but what method is going to be that
convenient for us?" Eva asked.

"Let me show you. We use this!" Pitohui replied. She stopped
running and smacked a small boat with a yellow cover right next
to the walkway.

From here to the stern of the ship, the rescue boats were packed
end to end.

"It's probably better if as many teams as possible rush the ship at
once from different directions, right, M?"

"That's right. So if you hear gunshots from some other team
getting to the ship, we'll go with that timing."

"What if everyone's thinking the same thing, so nobody
goes in?"

"It's possible. But the sea's rushing in on all of us, so everyone
has a time limit."

"Good point. Is it possible that as we get closer, other approaching teams will start a battle?"

"It's not impossible, but it seems like a bad idea."

"I guess so. Everyone wants on the ship first."

"And in that sense, it would be great if you could act as decoy,
Llenn. You can draw more gunshots than anyone else with your
presence."

"Sure, just give the order. I'll be your decoy."

Llenn and M were huddled on the field, planning their moves.
They were on their feet, ready to leap up and run the moment they
heard gunfire.

"Now?" asked Fukaziroh, who had her MGL-140s in either
hand and was dying to sprint. "Once we're within four hundred
yards, I'm gonna blast the hell out of 'em. It's just too bad I don't
have any smoke grenades this time!"

Fukaziroh had not brought any smoke grenades. She hadn't had the time to acquire any. If she'd brought them, she could have set up a smoke screen along the route to the ship, but it was too late to regret it now.

Instead, she had plasmas. Within her accuracy range, Fukaziroh's offensive power was unparalleled. She could aim for the upper parts of the ship and wreak untold destruction if she wanted.

"Not yet...?" Tanya murmured.

On the opposite side of the ship from Llenn's team—the southeast—SHINC was prepped and ready to charge the craft at any moment.

Their strategy was the same. Once they heard the sounds of battle, they would rush through the field, stick to the side of the ship, then go inside the holes they spotted with their binoculars.

"We've still got a hundred yards of space until the sea gets here," reported Anna, the rear guard. But there was no saying if the sea would pick up its pace.

"Not yet..."

Sophie prepped her left hand, ready to swing it at a moment's notice.

At this moment, MMTM and ZEMAL were also thinking the exact same thing.

And so was the audience in the bar. "Which is it? Which of them will jump first?"

On the monitors, they could see each team's hiding spot, as well as the waves coming for them.

"There's no way they'd all drown and let the betrayers' team win, right...?"

"Don't say that, man! I wanna see more battling! They set up this cruise ship; let's see some vacation combat!"

"Hang on. There's still the heavyweights from last time, T-S. My guess is that the sea level will go up until the ship is on water, but it'll still be below their rooftop area."

"Daaaah! Please, say it ain't so! What if the ship and building are miles away from each other?!"

"I dunno why you're asking me… Maybe the people who designed the map weren't thinking about that…"

Even the audience was worried about the future development of SJ3.

Then, at 1:08, there was movement—from the ship.

Llenn was the first to notice it.

"H…huh? Something fell from the ship. Something yellow."

M and Fukaziroh had been watching the side and rear. They snapped back to forward attention.

There, they saw a yellow-topped rescue boat falling from the starboard side of the mammoth cruise ship.

But those rescue boats belonged to a cruise ship that held thousands of passengers, so they were not small, by any means. The length of each one was well over seventy-five feet. In fact, they were larger than your average cruiser or fishing boat. Each one was meant to pack in the passengers when it was in use, with a capacity of over three hundred.

Those boats, hoisted to the side of the ship, were plummeting to the ground, one after the other. It was a drop of about fifty feet, where the boats crashed onto the grass.

The fiber-reinforced plastic must have deteriorated with age, because the bottom pieces cracked when they landed, making them useless as floating devices.

"Oh! They got us…," M gasped, a rare show of emotion.

"Huh? What are they doing?" Fukaziroh wondered idly.

They were watching the starboard side of the ship, but on the port side, the exact same thing was happening. Enormous rescue boats were dropping one after the other, starting near the prow.

"Agh! Shit!" said Jake, current leader of MMTM, as he looked through binoculars.

"Aaah! Oh no!" added Sophie from SHINC, from a separate location.

It took Llenn an extra beat to figure out the purpose of the people doing this.

When the boats fell and cracked onto the ground, they were covering up the holes on the side of the ship. In other words...

"Aaaah! Pito's blocking the holes we need to get inside!"

CHAPTER 12

There Is Still Time to Battle II

SECT.12

CHAPTER 12
There Is Still Time to Battle II

"Hoy!"

Pitohui swung her lightsword.

This was the one kind of sword that *for some reason* existed in the world of guns. It was a beam of light about three feet long that could cut through virtually any material. The strongest weapon imaginable—for a close-quarters fighter, that is.

Pitohui's pale-blue blade sliced through the thick wires holding the rescue boats aloft as smoothly as though they were nothing but thin air. Severing the front wires caused the boat to lose balance and tip forward. After cutting the few still holding it up in the back, it fell.

"There we go, there we go! We're closing up the entrances!"

She ran down the long deck, stopping and cutting as she went, dropping the rescue boats one after the other.

"Yo!"

On the other side of the ship, David, too, was cutting down the smaller boats off their wires. After dropping the third such boat to the ground below, his green-painted face split open to say "Next!"

He rushed to the adjacent boat, yelled "Raaah!" and simply sliced the thick crane frame that held the wires in the first place, rather than aiming at the smaller targets.

❊   ❊   ❊

Moments earlier, Pitohui was saying "Let me show you. We use this!" and slapping the plastic yellow roof of one of the rescue boats that lined the exterior walking deck.

"Huh?"

"What?" said Eva and David simultaneously. The other three just stared at Pitohui coldly, indicating that they did not grasp her point and needed her to elaborate.

"You don't get it?" she said. "It's so simple! We drop these down the side of the ship to block the entrance holes! Once we knock down all these ones lining the side, that'll eliminate a bunch of the places they can enter, right? And then all we have to do is protect the front and back!"

"That's true…," murmured Eva.

"I see. Okay, that makes sense," added David. "But do we have time to go lowering each and every one? If there's no power on board, we'll have to use the manual winch."

"Now, now, David. You need to fix that straightforward mind of yours. Who says we have to lower them the proper way?"

"Hey, shut up! So do you have a plan in mind?"

At last, Cole broke his silence to ask, "Blowing them up with our grenades, you mean?"

"*Bzzzt!* Wrong."

Next, Ervin gave it a guess. "Cutting the wires by shooting them?"

"No way! But you're close."

Lastly, Tomtom hoisted up his FN MAG and said, "I got it! You want us to break the crane arms by shooting them with a machine gun! I can do that!"

"Knock it off!" Pitohui said, pushing the muzzle down. "Ugh! You're all such pea-brained hotheads! Didn't you watch the video of the last time? Didn't you see my graceful close combat? In the log cabin!"

Her jaw hung open with disbelief. It was an expression she hardly ever made. Then she reached behind her back to pull out a lightsword from her pouch, the Muramasa F9. In its inactive state, it just looked like a piece of polished silver pipe.

"Ah, so you want to cut them down with that," Eva said in realization. "It'll be tough on your own, but good luck with that," she added, abdicating all responsibility.

"*Non-non-non!* We don't have time, so we need two people. I'll take starboard; David takes port."

"Wha—?!" David spluttered, stunned at being singled out. It was probably the biggest shock he'd experienced all day. "What the hell are you talking about, Pi—?"

"Come now, you don't think you can hide it from me, do you? You've got a lightsword, too!"

"……"

"After I skewered you like a sardine last time, you were so frustrated that you cried into your pillow every night, didn't you? You swore revenge, of course, so you paid through the nose to get one for yourself. So that if you got the chance, you could run me through with it!"

"……"

David said nothing.

"Is that true?" Ervin asked him.

"……"

After five seconds of silent trembling, David finally reached behind his back to pull out a gunmetal handle, extend its red blade, and shouted, "Port side!"

*   *   *

As the rescue boats dropped one after the other, M no longer had time to relax. "Llenn, Fuka, we're going. Jump out when I shoot. Zigzag randomly every three seconds. Fuka, once you get within range, shoot a grenade. Just hit the ship and make them back off. Llenn can rush in first."

At the very least, he wanted to attack the ship while the people dropping the boats were still busy with the task.

"R-roger that!"

"Roger!"

M crouched, took aim with the M14 EBR at the ship, which was within his effective range, and fired five times in quick succession.

Dam-dam-dam-dam-dam.

"Tah!"

"Let's go!"

The two diminutive girls burst out of the grassy area where they were hiding.

"Did you hear that? It's probably Llenn! Let's go!"

Gunfire was audible in the distance.

"Okay!"

"Charge!"

"About time!"

SHINC went on the move. Rosa fired her PKM machine gun for about three seconds for good measure, to act as a signal to the other squads.

"They're moving. Let's go!"

"Not that we have much of a choice!"

"Lightning speed!"

"Let's do it!"

MMTM's five went on the move.

And ZEMAL and TOMS. Each squad began to rush for the ship from their waiting locations.

The trio from TOMS didn't actually want to go in yet, because they were waiting for their comrade to do his dirty work, but if they waited around, they'd only drown, so they had little choice.

"Dammit!"

"Here they come!"

Ironically, it was Cole, the member from TOMS, who first

spotted the oncoming attackers. He was on lookout duty on Pito-hui's orders; he'd used his incredible agility to rush up stairs and ladders to the top of the mast at the very pinnacle of the ship. It was incredibly high, well above three hundred feet off the ground. There was a small lookout post with handrails just a handful of square feet in size, where he had a 360-degree view with his distance-measuring binoculars.

"Give me a report on location and features," Pitohui ordered. She was still cutting down more of the boats.

"The pink shrimp's on the fore starboard side. On the fore port side, the Amazons! Aft port looks like…MMTM, probably. That's ZEMAL directly to aft, and the aft starboard side is my old team!"

He hated to make things more dangerous for his buddies, but if he lied here, he would lose any trust he'd built up, so Cole accurately reported what he saw.

"Thanks! Just like the scan said!" Pitohui replied.

It occurred to Cole that if she knew what the scan said, shouldn't she also know where they were already? What was the point of him reporting to her?

Pitohui continued, "Now I know that the other teams aren't allied against us yet." It wasn't clear if she had read Cole's mind.

Ah, I see, he thought, ashamed of his lack of foresight. If multiple teams stormed the ship at once, that would require more bullets to shoot in different directions, giving each group a better chance of getting in. He should have realized that from the scan until now, the other squads might have teamed up and formed a truce until they could get on board.

That chick with the facial tattoos sure is smart, Cole thought. The potential opportunity to shoot such a powerful player in the back sent a thrill down his spine.

"I'm almost done here! How about you, Daveed?"

"You're going too fast! I'm only halfway done! And don't call me that!"

"Fine, fine, sorry. But if you don't hurry up, your ex-teammates will kill you. They're good at indoor combat, aren't they?"

"I know that!"

On the right and left sides of the huge ship, Pitohui and David ran and swung their lightswords. They could hear the sound of gunfire directed at the ship, but neither bullet lines nor bullets were reaching their area yet.

"Rah-rah-rah-rah-raaah!"

Blam-blam-blam-blam-blam-blam-blam-blam-blam-blam-blam!

Instead, they heard Tomtom's FN MAG blasting like crazy. He was on the stern deck with his machine gun propped on a bipod, shooting at the team approaching from the north. At ZEMAL, his old haunt.

"Feel my machine-gun love, you guyyyys! And if your machine-gun love is stronger than mine, lemme have iiiiit!" he roared.

Unfortunately, the other members of Team BTRY had no choice but to listen to him scream.

As the man's words came through his communications earpiece, Ervin thought, *Yep...that guy's crazy.*

And the other one is crazy, too.

In fact, are all the people on the betrayers' team crazy?

He was squatting on the deck, his XM8 resting snugly on the handrail in front of him. His current location was the fore starboard side of the ship, right before the helipad. The XM8's silencer was off, and its muzzle pointed in the direction of LPFM.

T-S's special helmets contained a distance readout. Ervin could also zoom in on his current image, so there was no need to pull it off to peer through binoculars if he wanted to see into the distance.

It seemed convenient, but it also meant that his ordinary vision was limited. So the helmet wasn't an all-around upgrade in that sense.

With his visuals zoomed in, he could see a small pink dot zipping across a field of grass. The distance measurement indicated she was still outside the effective range of his gun. He wanted to wait until she was within 450 yards.

The very next moment, a bullet came flying the other way without a bullet line.

Grnk!

It struck Ervin's head, clanked off with a few sparks and embedded into the ship exterior behind him to his left. A moment later, he heard the gunshot arrive.

The surprise of it all caused him to lose his balance and topple backward. "Whoa!"

But he did not lose any hit points.

Once M was within 750 yards of the ship, he stopped and sat flat on the ground. With his large backpack behind him for support, he placed the M14 EBR on top of his extended right knee and took careful aim at the man in the sci-fi armor.

The wind was completely still, so the bullet flew right where he aimed it. The shot hit the target in the head—but he bounced right back up, telling M that the bullet deflected. At this range, he couldn't shoot through that armor.

"It's tougher than I thought."

He'd watched the footage of the last Squad Jam for research, but there weren't any scenes of that team actually getting shot, so he didn't know what kind of defensive power they had. Now he did.

Perhaps it would be possible to damage his opponent's hit points by hitting the seams in the moving parts, like the back of the elbow and knee, but even M couldn't aim at something like that from this distance.

In fact, no player could pull off such a feat. It was already incredible that M could hit a target in one shot without bullet-circle assistance from over two thousand feet.

So M chose not to attempt it again. He lifted his considerable size up to his feet and resumed running. Somewhere ahead of him, Llenn and Fukaziroh were even closer to the ship.

"The closest one at this point is the pink shrimp! Five hundred yards!"

"Gotcha! I'm on it!" Pitohui replied to Cole, putting away her lightsword. She brought the KTR-09 around to her front and looked for the color pink on the fore side of starboard.

As soon as her eyes caught sight of it, she fired. It was a merciless, fully automatic assault. The bolt shot back and forth, expelling empties. The sound of gunfire rattled the glass of the ship's windows. It was only Pitohui's incredible strength that kept the powerful recoil from throwing off her aim.

I can do it! I can get there! Geez, that thing is huge, though...
Despite her shock at the size of the massive cruise ship, Llenn felt a burst of confidence. It was about four hundred yards away now. She'd been running zigzags, so she'd actually run much farther than that, but at this point, she started to think that she might make it if she just hurtled down the last stretch directly to the ship.

The rescue boats had fallen already, which meant that the only holes she could reach were near the prow, but with her group coming in at an angle, that was the closest spot already, so it wasn't a problem.

"We can do it! I'm gonna rush straight for it, M!" she called out.
Immediately, he replied, "Stop! Pito's aiming at you!"

He was keeping watch from the rear. If he hadn't said that, Llenn would have continued running straight forward.

And one of the hail of lines and bullets that proceeded would have pierced her body, without a doubt.

"Hyaaaaaa!"
Like a dog that suddenly spotted a more fearsome adversary, Llenn reacted to the arrival of the grass-sprayed bullets by spinning around on the spot, three whole times.

Fukaziroh saw her do it from the rear. "Ooh, that was cute."

*   *   *

"The little pink one's spinning around," Cole reported.

"Okay! It's all you now, Ervin. You don't actually have to hit her. Just spray full auto in her general area. Use the bullet lines as cover to keep her at bay."

"G-got it! I think I can handle that!"

"Good luck, then!" Pitohui said, swinging the KTR-09 back behind her and drawing her lightsword again. She resumed the process of knocking down the rescue boats.

With her encouragement, Ervin aimed his XM8 at the pink dot and began spraying bullets.

"Shit! I can't get any closer!"

Llenn's scheme was at a halt. There were still at least 450 yards to the ship. The red lines and the bullets that created them were flying fast and thick, and it was all she could do to avoid them.

Given the higher-pitched sound and the particular qualities of the ballistic arc, she could tell that the shots coming from near the prow of the ship belonged to a 5.56 mm assault rifle. They flew fast and curved, before dropping down at the very end.

If she got any closer, her chances of getting hit increased significantly. In the switchyard, it was easier to dodge because she could run in any direction, but it was harder now that she had to go one particular way.

The bullets were right at effective firing range, so now that her hit points were back to full, there might not be a concern about a one-hit kill—but if she fell and got picked off by a sniper, that would really suck.

"Fuka? Can you get a shot onto the ship?" she asked Fukaziroh, who was about fifty yards behind her.

"Hmm, it's still a bit far. They'll drop right in front of it. And the thing is, wasted ammo doesn't really suit me."

"Can you come up a bit farther, then? I really think you're the kind of lady who shines at the front of the stage, Fuka!"

"I appreciate the attempt to flatter me, but that's not happening. I'm not as fast as you, Llenn, so I could get shot before I get that chance to shine."

"Ugh," Llenn grunted, dodging bullets. She tried M next. "M, can you snipe that guy from where you are?"

"I already did."

"Oh? And…?"

"He's covered in armor. I hit him, but the bullets just bounce off."

Oh, it's them! Or one of them, I guess! Llenn thought.

"Oh, it's them! Or one of them, I guess!" Fukaziroh said at the exact same moment. They were in perfect synchronization.

It was clear they still felt they had a score to settle.

Eighteen hundred feet to the ship.

M dropped down and got into sniping position again. With the scope at full zoom, the man in the sci-fi armor was much larger than before.

Blam-blam.

He fired two shots in quick succession. Sparks flew on the man's right elbow and left arm.

"I tried some covering snipes. Will that make him back off?" he said to Llenn and Fukaziroh. If it freaked out the guy and got him to take cover, the girls would be able to rush closer, making their progress much easier.

But the shots still issued from the ship. The man was firmly in place along the edge of the ship deck. He continued firing, ignoring the shots his armor was taking.

"Guess not."

As long as they don't shoot my gun! Ervin thought, his heart jackhammering away in his chest.

He was sitting cross-legged at the rim of the ship, the end of the XM8's body resting on the handrail, keeping his gun facing the enemy as best he could. That was to make his gun's target as small as possible. With the shield on his left hand, it could guard against attacks from the side angle, too. While there was armor all over his body, M's 7.62 mm shots clanging off his frame and head were nothing short of pure horror. The armor blocked the bullet, but the impact still transferred through, and depending on the spot, it might register as a physical blow and lower his HP.

But if he put his body on the line and stuck this one out, he would be able to prevent the fearsome LPFM from getting closer to the ship.

And even if he was aligned with a different team at the moment, he was executing T-S's battle style.

I'm the defending champion! Even if I got lucky through particular circumstances!

Ervin kept firing the XM8, even as it got overheated and smoke began to trickle out of the barrel.

"Okay, dropped them all off the starboard side!" Pitohui reported, turning off her lightsword and returning it to the pouch on her back. She took off running.

"Amazons coming from the left! Five hundred yards!" Cole told her.

"Got it! Coming to back up!"

She sprinted along the starboard deck toward the prow. After about a thousand feet, she crossed over through an interior hallway to the port side, back to the space just before the helipad.

Eva was there, but her Vintorez only had an effective range of about 450 yards, so she'd only be wasting bullets. Instead, she occasionally peeked out from the thick metal lip of the ship deck, wary of shots from Anna's and Tohma's Dragunovs.

"Hey, there! Not happy about shooting your friends?"

"That would be inaccurate."

Pitohui slipped past Eva's side to the wall, placed her KTR-09 atop it, and opened a merciless round of automatic gunfire.

The bullets showered down on the rest of SHINC, who were within about five hundred yards at this point.

Through sheer coincidence—presumably—one of Pitohui's bullets happened to catch Rosa's thigh as she ran.

"Gah!" She toppled, rolling over her PKM. "Shit!"

Anna dropped to a sitting position on the ground, avoiding any bullet lines in the area. She swept the Dragunov's aim toward the flash of gunfire from the ship's port side, but the other person had ducked back behind cover.

Three seconds later, there was more gunfire from a slightly different spot. Anna didn't have time to relax and snipe; she had to roll around to dodge the shot.

"Whoever that is, they're tough. Who is it?" she shouted.

"Well, it's definitely not Boss. I heard the shots," replied Tanya, who ducked and wove as she ran.

"Yaaah! There, that's all of them!"

On the port side, David finished dropping the last of the rescue boats. That meant there wouldn't be any place to get onto the ship aside from the prow and the stern. It also meant there were no more rescue boats to be used.

"Rear left! Camo team incoming! Within four hundred yards!" Cole reported.

"I'll handle them!" David said. He swung his weapon, an STM-556 with a long barrel attached, into firing position.

Damn that dirty Pitohui! She arranged us so we'd each be attacking our old teams! He swore as he sprinted a distance of about a hundred feet. Along the way, he fired the grenade launcher attached to the bottom of his gun.

"Launcher!"

The fat, arcing bullet line was evidence of a grenade launcher being deployed.

At Kenta's warning, the rest of the team looked to the air to confirm the spot of the line, then threw themselves flat on the ground. Even if it wasn't touching them, being too close to the landing point could easily put them within lethal range of grenade shrapnel. The only defense against such a thing was to hit the dirt.

Ba-gomp!

The grenade exploded almost in the center of the formation of four.

"Damn, that was close!"

Dirt and grass kicked up by the explosion pattered down atop Summon, the closest to the blast. If he'd kept running, he would have gotten lacerated by the shrapnel right next to him.

"Launcher!"

Another came flying toward them just three seconds later. This one was going to hit Bold flush on the chest.

"Dwayaaa!" he yelped. If he didn't leap to his feet and run at top speed, it would have obliterated his avatar.

Bold escaped instant death, but some of the shrapnel bit into his back. Meanwhile, sniper shots were coming in hot, one after the other.

"Gah!"

One hit his stomach, knocking him over and stealing about 40 percent of his hit points.

Desperate to keep his gun from suffering damage, Jake went to lie down on top of the HK21 machine gun and screamed, "Launcher sniper combo!"

Using the narrow window after the grenade blast from the launcher to get into stable sniping position and pick off the targets as they tried to evade the blast was David's forte.

"That's our team leader! Oh, dammit! Of all the shitty luck!" Jake swore.

"You're wrong about that. *You're* the leader now, man. Ah-ha-ha-ha-ha," teased Kenta.

"Daaah! This isn't time for jokes!"

"Well, how can you not laugh?!"

"……"

Lux listened to his teammates' argument and moved slowly, ever so slowly, over the grass. He was the member farthest to the rear—and outside the grenade launcher's range. The opponent, however, was inside his MSG90's range.

He set it against his shoulder and, moving slowly enough to hopefully avoid attention, pointed it at the cruise ship's rear.

His view through the scope caressed the ship as it sought its prey, until…

"Damn…"

He did not succeed in finding the enemy lying in wait.

The ship was simply too big, and there were too many places to hide.

"MMTM has stopped to the rear left! The water's up to about seven hundred yards! It's looking good!" announced Cole, who was peering through his binoculars. At his hip, the MP7A1 bounced with excitement.

Cole hadn't shot once since getting on the ship, because he was undertaking the most important task of all.

"Good job, Cole!" Pitohui said encouragingly.

"Thanks!" he said automatically, then chided himself for it. *Don't get all chummy now. The point isn't for us to go on and win… I gotta find some way to betray them already…*

In the meantime, he simply prayed that his teammates wouldn't die until then. Although he was supposed to be watching in all 360 degrees, Cole couldn't help but glance aft a bit more often, in the direction of his original squad.

In that aft direction, which was north, two teams encountered each other in a grassy field about 1,600 feet away.

Three speedy fellows in light gear—namely, TOMS—rushed over to their nearest neighbors, ZEMAL.

"Hey! Don't shoot, don't shoot!" they cried, lifting up their arms and pointing their guns away.

"Wha—?"

ZEMAL had been making their way through the field, dodging gunfire from their former teammate, but they did come to a stop now. They hadn't noticed the other team approaching at all, so TOMS could have opened fire on them if they wanted. Maybe they wouldn't have gotten all four ZEMAL members, but they certainly might have finished off two. But in a direct firefight with the remaining two, they would lose.

Separated by twenty yards, the two groups crouched in the grass and held a conference, rather than a conflict.

The leader of TOMS, who used the HK53, shouted, "Let's attack the stern together!"

ZEMAL's acting leader, Huey, with the M240B, replied, "What do you mean?"

"You get it, don't you? If we don't get inside that ship, we're all gonna drown pretty soon! We survived this far; that's no warrior's way to go out, is it? So let's have a truce until we can get on the ship!"

Even as they spoke, the water was getting closer to their position. These were the two teams farthest from the ship at the moment. In other words, they were the closest to the waves. They probably had a hundred feet of dry land to work with now, if that.

And of course, Tomtom was keeping them at bay. He kept spraying them with bullets from high up on the ship deck, which prevented them from moving quickly. There was nothing quite like a machine gun for holding back an entire plane of space at once.

Of course, ZEMAL knew they were facing their old teammate, and they gave it back to him whenever they could—but Tomtom would just slip away from their bullet lines, pop up somewhere else, and resume blasting at them.

Huey said to the TOMS leader, "I see, I see. I get what you're saying. By the way, you guys like machine guns?"

"Huh…? Not really, we live for speed. I'm afraid I don't go for heavy guns."

"Then we can't fight with you. We can't be friends with you.

And if you're not friends, you're enemies. I'll need you to die. That's what my machine gun's whispering to me."

"Whaaaat?!" the TOMS leader yelped.

Blam-blam-blam-blam-blam-blam-blam-blam-blam!

His voice was drowned out by machine-gun fire from very close by. The four members of ZEMAL stood up and unloaded the maximum firepower of their machine guns. No one could escape that kind of lead shower in a field without solid cover.

They could outrun many things, but not that.

"Hya-hya-hya! They started shooting *now*?!"

"Yeah! Don't forget, it's a battle royale!"

"Way to go, you machine-gun freaks!"

Cheers erupted in the pub at the sight of TOMS going out in a true warrior's blaze of glory.

"Wha—?! Wha—?! Whyyyyyyyyyyyy?!"

Cole screamed at the sight of TOMS being obliterated in the distance. Through his binoculars, he could see his three "team-mates" lighting up with red bullet-wound effects, being turned into Swiss cheese, and toppling to the grass like rags.

It was the machine gunners they'd been talking to mere moments before who shot them. In other words, it was a negotiation that turned into a murder scene. A cowardly sneak attack—at least, in Cole's mind.

"You'll pay for thiiiiiiiis!"

Who *wouldn't* scream at a situation like this? Not him.

"What is it?" Pitohui said through the comm, her voice calm and quiet. Cole couldn't give her a straight answer.

"Dammit… Those bastards," he grunted, glaring aft.

"Ah, your old pals got done in. Pour one out if you must, but don't just stare at the rear, or you'll die. Watch the entire perimeter for bullet lines," Pitohui warned him.

What? Lines? Cole thought. *But I'm right at the top of the middle of the ship. No one's going to be able to aim at me all the way up here, you dumb broad! Forget it, I'm going down so I can kill them all! In onboard combat, my agility and small, versatile weapon will serve me best of all! I'm gonna do this! I'm gonna kill all the rest of them!*

Obviously, if he said a word of this out loud, they would hear him in their earpieces, so he had to keep it in his mind.

So Cole was already sulking and thinking about his revenge—but if he had watched out as she warned him, he would have easily seen the bullet line sticking into his midriff.

An enormous 14.9 mm bullet came roaring at him over an incredibly long distance, honing in on Cole's right torso. On impact, the kinetic energy cascaded through his body, sending it bulging outward. And when the flesh was unable to withstand the pressure, it burst.

The upper half of the man atop the lookout post exploded from within.

His hands, head, and MP7A1 all fell in different places.

Team BTRY's first casualty was dead before he knew what hit him.

The rumble of SHINC's secret weapon, the anti-tank PTRD-41 rifle, boomed like thunder. It was audible from anywhere on the ship.

Pitohui saw her teammate's hit points drop in the corner of her view and she spat, "Ugh, dammit! I just warned him! Cole's dead. Our eyes are gone, everyone."

"Yes! Brilliant shot! Well done," said Sophie, who sat cross-legged with her shoulder as a gun stand.

"Phew..." Tohma, the sniper who'd hit her long-distance target in one shot, sighed.

They were directly even with the middle of the ship on the port side, at a distance of 1,300 feet.

Earlier, they'd broken off from the other members and gone directly north. That was so they could defeat the person on lookout duty atop the ship, of course. If he wasn't reporting to the others, approaching the ship would be easier—for SHINC and for the other squads.

But that required getting closer to the target. From a diagonal, they couldn't reach the top of the 1,600-foot ship. They had to be perpendicular for the best distance.

While their teammates shot and scampered and drew attention, somehow the other two managed to slip away undetected. Sophie pulled the PTRD-41 out of her inventory. Tohma set up to fire but did not put her finger on the trigger. If it created a bullet line, their target would move out of the way.

The man was constantly turning, checking different directions. It seemed like they might not get a chance to shoot him. The sea was approaching from behind.

Suddenly, they got their first and last opportunity.

He stared at the stern of the ship and froze.

Tohma calmly, carefully, took aim and fired.

And killed him.

Now the water was fifteen feet behind them and getting closer.

"Five shots left. What now?" Tohma asked.

Sophie gave her a smile. "Hey, it's a big target. If you just want to shoot it, I can do that, too."

"Then...I'll get going. See you later." Tohma grinned back, then took off at a sprint with her Dragunov in one hand.

She looked back over her shoulder for only one second and saw Sophie getting to her feet, holding the shoulder bag with the five shots in it. Next, she picked up the PTRD-41 in her right hand. The place where the bag had been resting one instant earlier was now underwater.

Sophie placed the tip of the long gun barrel against the grass, loaded the next bullet with her other hand, and cycled the big, heavy bolt.

As the ocean water engulfed her legs, the dwarf woman's large body held the long, heavy gun at waist level. As though she were prepping a spear.

Her target: the ship. A large, wavering bullet circle appeared to no one but her. She placed it over the boat.

Kablam.

The gun fired, the recoil lowering the bolt and expelling the empty cartridge. A huge shower of sparks appeared against the side of the ship.

She reloaded.

Kablam.

She reloaded.

Kablam.

She reloaded...

"Guess this is it... Good luck, everyone. Good luck, Boss."

The water was up to her waist now. She couldn't shoot anymore. As her body went farther under the water, the loss of hit points grew faster.

At last, the salt water rose over her head, and she sank without a sound, never letting go of the gun.

*   *   *

"Found him!"

Just a little bit earlier in time, less than a minute before Cole got shot, Lux the sniper was desperate to catch a glimpse of David.

On a balcony three floors up from the promenade deck in a section of cabins near the stern, a gun muzzle could be faintly seen through broken window glass.

Lux did not hesitate. "Once I shoot, everyone else go! Full sprint! Get there!"

"Huh? What are you gonna do?" Kenta asked.

"I'm gonna hold Team Leader down," he replied without missing a beat. "Otherwise, we're all gonna drown or get blown up."

"No, wait. *You're* gonna drown, man! Have you looked behind you?"

"Yeah."

"Then you know that's not the answer!"

"But if Team Leader were here, that's what he'd order, isn't it?"

"......Yeah, I guess you're right... Fine, I'll do it."

*   *   *

The MSG90 emitted a high-pitched bark.

The 7.62 mm bullet it shot flew into the ship.

"Gah!"

David avoided the line, but it did manage to take a two-inch chunk out of his right arm. He lost 7 percent of his hit points in the process. Only by spinning and flipping over did he evade the second and third bullets that came in the same spot.

"Nice shooting, Lux!" he marveled. "Tomtom, lay down fire on the port side, aft! Watch out for the sniper!"

He needed some extra firepower from the one other teammate who could hit his side of the ship—but there was no response.

"Tomtom?"

*   *   *

Blam-blam-blam-blam-blam-blam-blam-blam-blam-blam.

Again, earlier—less than a minute before Cole got shot— Tomtom was blasting away with his FN MAG to keep his former squadmates from getting closer.

Blam-blam-blam-blam-blam… Click.

He ran out of ammo.

The very long ammunition belt hanging from the left side of the machine gun had been depleted at last.

"Whoopsie. Reload time," he said happily, pulling the back-pack off his shoulder and squatting to look inside it.

A single bullet hurtled toward him and pierced his bandana.

"Gah?"

His head went limp and plonked directly into the opened back-pack. He did not move again.

"Wha—? Was that my bullet?" wondered Shinohara as he lowered the M60E3 from his shoulder.

"Yep, that hit him! Nice one!" said Max, the black member

with the Minimi, who was watching through binoculars. "You beat the 'enemy' team's machine gunner!"

"Whoooooooooo!"

"We beat the toughest enemy there iiiiis!"

The four men roared and cheered, their bodies glowing with damage effects from shots they'd taken. Peter, the one with the tape over his nose, even let loose with his Negev into the air.

Then their erstwhile leader, tough-guy Huey, asked, "So…what now?"

"It's kinda boring once you beat the toughest enemy. Do we even care about conquering the ship?"

"Nah, I don't really feel like going through all that. What should we do now?"

"Wanna have fun on our own?"

"Yeah, that sounds better."

"Agreed."

The crowd in the pub couldn't believe their eyes.

"……"

The members of ZEMAL were cavorting around in the field. They were running, chasing after one another. Shooting at one another.

Bullets were flying in every direction at the rear of the ship. Tracer rounds left dazzling lines of light that sprayed out with no rhyme or reason.

One of them went down. Then a second. His smile was dazzling, as innocent as a child's. The survivors' legs splashed in the water, but they kept shooting. Then the third one went down, and the last remaining man raised his arms in a victory pose, shooting into the air.

It was in that pose that he quietly sank beneath the water.

"……"

The crowd in the pub couldn't believe their eyes.

CHAPTER 13

Close-Quarters Battle

SECT.13

CHAPTER 13
Close-Quarters Battle

When Pitohui saw Tomtom's HP bar vanish in the corner of her vision, she lamented, "Awww! I guess that's the end of our defensive line."

She made eye contact with Eva, who was lying behind cover about ten yards away. They were on their bellies on the helipad, while the bullet lines from Rosa's PKM vanished as her shots flew over their heads.

"You're going to let the enemy onto the ship?" Eva asked.

"That's right," Pitohui promptly replied. "We should meet up and retreat before we lose any more team members. We've done quite well so far."

On the rear port side, David was stuck behind cover, due to the watchful eye of Lux. "And that'll put us back into a proper battle-royale configuration. Works for me," he agreed.

MMTM would be very close to the ship by now, and even if he could peek out and get some shots off, he wouldn't be able to take out all of them. Though Lux, who was keeping him stuck in place, was likely to stay out there and die in the water before he could get to safety.

The bastards got me, David thought proudly. The ship combat that was to come would involve very short distances, which meant the expertise of a sniper was very limited.

By sacrificing himself and ensuring that the other four with machine guns and assault rifles got on board, he maximized the team's chances. David would have signed off on such a strategy if he were there.

"Where should we rendezvous?" he asked.

"Let's go to the bridge. Did you hear that, Ervin?"

"Ah yes!"

"You don't have to come to the port side. Just spray one last magazine, then come inside. Go up the stairs, to the highest deck, all the way to the front."

"G-got it."

Ervin was on the starboard side focusing mightily on the pink dot. He let loose with thirty more shots, not bothering to aim too hard, then stood and ran from the spot. M got off another shot at him, but it only bounced off his shoulder protector.

"The enemy's pulled back! Run, you two! No need to shoot."

"Roger that!"

"Got it."

Llenn and Fukaziroh zoomed across the field. A little over four hundred yards remained. If there wasn't going to be any attacking, they could just make a straight beeline for it.

"I'll be along right behind you," M continued. He began running after them, holding his M14 EBR in front. The water was already over his ankles at this point.

His running speed and the advancing speed of the sea were the same. On the monitors in the bar, it was clear that he was desperately moving his large body as fast as it would go, yet, there was no difference in his position and the water's edge. It was like some kind of visual illusion. The crowd was fully engaged.

"Whoa, is he gonna make it?"

"Hurry! Hurry!"

"M! I know you're not the kind of guy who dies here!"

Different monitors displayed the whereabouts of BTRY. First

was Cole, whose face was sleeping and peaceful in death. After he'd been blown apart, his corpse reconstituted atop the mast.

Next was Tomtom, who was unmoving on the rear deck, his head stuck inside his backpack on the ground, like some weird art installation.

Of the remaining four, Pitohui and Eva were climbing stairs inside the ship. This was the audience's first view of the ship's interior. It was filthy with age, but the power was still on, so it was fully illuminated.

David was running at full speed through the huge, lengthy courtyard area in the middle of the ship.

And Ervin's bulky, armored body was running down a tight hallway, bouncing awkwardly off obstacles here and there.

The first to get inside the ship were the four remaining members of MMTM.

Kenta the G36K user was the first to reach the hole. Wary of what might be inside, he opened his inventory window as he ran and attached a powerful flashlight to the left side of his gun.

That was in expectation that the interior would be dark, but in fact, there were LED lights strung up every few yards on the inside. They must have hung them up when escaping the ship originally.

"We've got light inside. Pile in, guys!"

"Got it!" said Bold.

"You bet," followed Summon.

"Whew…made it," said Jake, bringing up the rear with his machine gun.

The quartet of MMTM rushed in through the hole.

About ten seconds later, four members of SHINC made it inside.

In the lead, of course, was Tanya, their point person. She entered with her silenced Bizon steadied at her shoulder; it barely swayed as she walked.

It was unlikely that any of the enemies who'd been shooting from the deck dozens of feet above would suddenly be down there, but it never hurt to be cautious.

Anna followed, pushing the slower Rosa, and turned back to yell "Hurry, Tohma!"

Tohma had been the farthest back, so she could shoot the PTRD-41, and was still running to catch up to the group. The sea was right on her heels—but Tohma was fairly quick, and her boots never got wet.

"Whew! Thanks for waiting! Give the orders now, Rosa!"

Llenn's foot speed was the fastest of all surviving players. As she sprinted, the huge white structure grew larger and larger, until it was looming over her head.

"It's massive..."

When Llenn—make that Karen—was in elementary school, she once took a ferry trip from Otaru Port in Hokkaido to Maizuru Port all the way down in Kyoto. It was during a family vacation to Kyoto.

The name of the ship was the *Hanamasu*.

According to its catalog, it was a bit under 730 feet long. When she and her sister gazed up at it from Otaru, it looked enormous. The space on board was stunning. She could go around searching every nook and cranny, and it would never end. It tuckered her out.

That memory was a vivid one for her, but the ship she saw now was over twice the size of the ferry. If she kept looking up at it, she felt she would flip over backward. Since she was near its prow, if she looked to the side, the stern was impossibly distant. She couldn't see where it ended.

"It's *too* massive..."

What was happening on this ship? She'd have to fight enemy squads on board? And she had to find Pitohui in the process?

Thinking about all the challenges she had to juggle was making her woozy.

Once she was at the edge of the mountain-like ship, Llenn pointed her P90 at the hole before her. Part of the hole was underground at this point, but it was still large enough for a person to pass through, even one the size of M.

It looked like it had been forcefully, violently burned through the metal. On the inside was another layer of steel with the same hole through it. Beyond that, she could see hanging LED lights. No sign of any human presence.

Llenn turned back. Fukaziroh had started running from about the same spot, so she was close enough that her face was recognizable. Her dual MGL-140s were resting on her shoulders as she ran along, chanting like some kind of Edo-era palanquin bearer.

"Ei-ho! Ei-ho!"

Behind her was nothing but green grass and gray seawater and, in the distance, the small form of M.

"You can do it, M!"

"What, no words of encouragement for me? I feel so left out. I'm gonna sulk now."

"You've got plenty of time, Fuka! I'm worried about M!"

Fukaziroh turned to look at M behind her as she ran. "Good point... M, do you want me to end it all for you? I can shoot you. It's cooler to get blown up than to drown, don't you think?"

"Fuka!"

"I'm just trying to lighten the mood with a joke. I'm not gonna shoot him. Ei-ho! Ei-ho!" Fukaziroh said. She reached Llenn within a few more seconds. "Phew! I'm tired! Mentally."

Both Llenn and Fukaziroh waited for M outside the ship. He could see them from his distant position, and he yelled, "Go in!"

"But—!"

"There's no point if we *all* drown!"

"C'mon, you know M's right," said Fukaziroh, cool and collected. She started to go through the hole, but Llenn grabbed her arm.

"Wait!"

"C'mon, I don't want to do a romantic group suicide. You know that Pito is smiling and waiting for us up there. There's nothing left for us to do down here. We're nothing more than useless low-lifes whose only skills are shooting guns."

"That's it! Fuka...prepare to fire Leftania!"

"Huh?"

"Oh, he's not gonna make it..."

"Yeah... Is this it for M?"

The audience in the pub had a bird's-eye view, so they could see the situation very well. Perhaps because the higher part of the island was also rather flat, the approach of the water was much faster now. In other words, it was no longer keeping pace with M's top speed, but it was moving faster than he was toward the ship.

"Won't the girls be in trouble if they don't go inside the ship, too? There's no guarantee that there are stairs right inside the hole, is there?"

"Exactly. And the water's going to rush into the ship, obviously..."

They were very concerned about Llenn and Fukaziroh. Meaning that they'd already given up on M. It looked like the sea was picking up speed. He had about 250 feet to go, but there was no way he'd make it in time.

In another five seconds, M's large body would be swallowed up by the enormous gray slime that was the ocean.

"Good-bye, M... We'll never forget your heroic combat ability... Amen...," said someone in the crowd. Just then, the ocean blew up.

"Huh?"

The giant slime exploded, right behind M.

No, it wasn't the ocean that exploded...

"A plasma grenade!"

It was an explosive that created a brilliant-blue vortex of energy. The plasma grenade's blast diameter was twenty yards

across. Everything within that range was obliterated and sent flying outward.

Including enemies and even seawater.

"One more, Fuka!"

"You got it!"

Pomp.

Fukaziroh's left-hand MGL-140 shot out another blue projectile.

Since the target was close, it shot at a low angle, barely passing over M's head and exploding only twenty-five yards behind him.

Another blue orb erupted within the rushing sea. The blast pushed against M's back.

"I can't believe you thought of this...," Fukaziroh gasped.

"See? You've got something to do after all, don't you?" Llenn grinned.

The audience watched as two successive plasma-grenade blasts succeeded at bringing the seawater to a halt directly behind M.

Right after the surge of the explosions finished, the water rushed back from the sides and rear, but there was also a big hole gouged out of the ground, so the force was not enough to hit M and drag him away.

Llenn and Fukaziroh vanished into the hole in the ship just before M got there. He plunged through the opening at a full run.

Three seconds after the last member of the team disappeared from view, the water smashed against the hull of *There Is Still Time*.

Their crisis continued.

They were inside the ship but still at the same level as the water. Fortunately, or perhaps by design, just a few yards after getting through the hole in the outer ship wall, there was a hallway with a narrow staircase.

"Hurry and climb!"

"Hyaaaa!"

"C'mon, Llenn, go! Or we'll run over you!"

Under the bright light of the LEDs, Llenn sped up the stairs, Fukaziroh clunked and clonked the walls with her bulky grenade launchers, and last came M, hunching his large body as he climbed.

Once Llenn had gone up five stories' worth, she came to a large mirror and a door. A figure appeared in the mirror.

"Eep!" Llenn flinched and even pointed the P90 at the mirror.

"Hey, it's me!"

In English, the mirrored door said GUEST FLOOR AHEAD, CHECK YOUR APPEARANCE. She pushed it open.

If anyone was there, they'd be an enemy, and she would have opened fire, but there was no one. It was just a slightly larger hallway, about five feet wide and seven and a half feet high, certainly not what anyone would call spacious. Even on a luxury cruise ship, internal space was at a premium.

The floor was covered in thick carpet. It was faded and flattened, of course. The wallpaper was once off-white, but now it was either degraded or peeling everywhere.

The hallway was straight and very long. There was nothing in it. It was so long, in fact, that no one could see to the end. The lights on the ceiling continued all the way down.

Behind her, it went about seventy feet to a dead end. There were doors on either wall set at regular intervals. That meant this was the lowest of the passenger cabin decks, on the right side of the ship, near the front.

Fukaziroh reached the hallway, then M arrived after her, and they closed the door firmly.

"Thanks. You two saved me," M said, heaving a deep breath to ease his agitation.

"Are we safe here? Will the water come up?" Llenn wondered.

"We should be fine for a while. First the water will flood into the lower sections, bit by bit. But before that—" Suddenly a sound cut M off.

Grurrrrurrurrurrrrrrg.

It was a sound like the growling of some mammoth beast, and it seemed to envelop them from the outside. It continued without stopping, until Fukaziroh said, "What's this? Are we in the belly of some beast?"

"No. But the ship is groaning."

"Why?"

"It must be happy."

"Excuse me? Don't treat it like a person. Again, why?" Fukaziroh repeated.

For some reason, M sounded pleased. "It gets to be a ship again."

The best vantage point for the situation, as usual, belonged to the audience watching from the safety of the pub. They were practically omniscient.

Immediately after M vanished into the ship, a huge amount of seawater enveloped its sides. The gray water went into the hole, of course, but the overall level quickly rose above it, so the hole was entirely hidden from view.

The rescue boats that Pitohui and David cut down simply sank rather pathetically. They certainly couldn't float with their bottoms completely cracked from the fall. Instead, the boats' equipment, like red-and-white life buoys and orange-painted boxes, floated unescorted to the surface like trash.

The water level rose and rose against the side of the cruise ship.

"Hang on. If the water keeps rising at this pace, the whole thing's gonna be submerged within minutes. Everyone's gonna die, y'know?" someone shrieked.

"That's not happening, idiot," another watcher snapped.

"What makes you so sure?"

"So what if there are holes? It's a ship. What do you think happens when a ship is surrounded by water?"

As if in response to the question, the cruise ship budged. Suddenly, the water level rising against its side slowed. It stopped. Then it began to lower.

"Whoa!"

The diagonal aerial angle made it very clear. The enormous ship was slowly but surely rising within the water.

The part of the ship that was buried under the ground began to pull free with the power of the craft's buoyancy. Dirt flooded the churning water around the base, and a great amount of grass floated to the surface.

Finally, the ship rose up high upon the water, then sank a bit and stabilized.

At last, the ship was a ship again.

"It's floating!"

"Hya-hoo!"

"Onward!"

The audience cheered and roared, although they were nowhere near the actual ship.

It was 1:15. In an hour and fifteen minutes, the island six miles to a side had completely sunk beneath the waves. Now it was replaced by a new battlefield, 550 yards long and a hundred yards wide.

This was the final round of third Squad Jam.

At that point, only the bar audience had a precise knowledge of who made it to the final stage—which teams were left, and how many members each had.

There were four teams atop the ship.

First, the team made up of traitors from the other squads, Betrayers (BTRY).

Pitohui, David, Ervin, Eva.

Three assault rifles, one with a grenade launcher attached. One silenced sniper rifle. The Vintorez could fire full auto, though, so one might say they had four assault rifles.

Memento Mori (MMTM) had Kenta, Bold, Summon, and Jake.

Three assault rifles and one machine gun.

SHINC had Anna, Tohma, Rosa, and Tanya.

That was two snipers, one machine gunner, and one attacker with a submachine gun.

Lastly, LPFM had only three left, one fewer than the others: Llenn, M, Fukaziroh.

That was one attacker, one sniper, and one rapid-firing grenadier.

"If you were gonna bet on one of these teams, which would it be?"

An impromptu betting pool surfaced among the audience.

"I'm going Team Betrayers all the way. You got three ridiculously powerful players, *and* they've got the high ground!"

"I'd say MMTM. You saw their fight inside the spaceship in the first Squad Jam, right? They're unstoppable in close quarters!"

"Yeah, but SHINC's got a chance, too. If they can get into combat in the open, the combo of a machine gun and two snipers will keep anyone else away, plus they have a free-roaming attacker, too."

There was clear personal preference and optimism at play, but each opinion had its logical backing.

"So who's gonna bet on Llenn's team to win?"

The bar went silent.

"What, nobody? The first champion and second runner-up?" the same person teased.

"I dunno, pink pip-squeak aside, their speed isn't going to get them through this, right?"

"The grenadier's got too much power; she can't shoot indoors. There's no point to her fighting up close. She'll only be in the way."

"M's size is going to be a disadvantage. He'll fill the entire hallway with a target when he walks. And because of the terrain, he won't have time and space to set up his perfect shield wall, I bet."

The nitpicks and quibbles came fast and furious. In the end, nobody would put their money where their mouth was for Llenn's team.

The bridge of the ship was at the top of the structure and right at the front, bulging outward like a pop-eyed goldfish. It was about the size of a school classroom, rather compact for a ship this enormous. The floor was covered in thin carpet for good traction, and the outward window was spacious and curved for visibility.

Despite being the "bridge" of the ship, the only actual controls in the room were inside the console area, a three-sided section maybe sixteen feet to a side, with a number of monitors raised above the controls.

There were only six chairs in the room. Thanks to modernized automation, such ships could run on a shockingly small number of crew members, so that was all it needed. The rest of the bridge space was for visitors, if passengers wanted to come and observe.

And in the center of the console area, slightly higher than the others, was the fancy captain's chair. In front of that, right before the window, was the helmsman's seat with the ship's wheel.

It was easy to imagine a ship having a giant wheel, but in recent days, they'd been designed so small that they looked like toys. This one wasn't even as large as a truck's steering wheel.

This ship had been dormant for so long that the bridge room changed over time, rusting and dirty here and there, but nothing seemed to be broken. Even the window glass was still perfectly intact.

But none of the ceiling lights were on. The many monitors were silent. And of course, there was no one in the room.

Then footsteps approached the bridge. The double doors were violently kicked open from outside.

The four members of Team BTRY came stomping into the bridge: Pitohui, Eva, David, and Ervin.

Instantly, the LED lights flickered on. Ervin even tensed, thinking in the moment that it was an enemy attack.

Then the console monitors popped on. The ship was still operational, in fact.

"Human response detected in bridge," said a voice. It was a relaxed female voice, but they could tell it did not belong to a human.

Pitohui stood in front of the console and said, "Hi! I'm Pitohui."

"Greetings, Pitohui and company. This is the main computer of There Is Still Time. *I have been given a nickname. Please call me Clara. I welcome you to our control room. Please give me any instructions you have."*

The other three were quietly stunned. In *GGO*, they'd seen many Earth-made machines that had gone haywire and attacked them. They were common enemies to destroy or be killed by in the game.

But this was absolutely the first time they'd come across a machine that obeyed human commands. Obviously, it was only because this was under the unique circumstances of the Squad Jam event.

"Hi, Clara. Can you sail us?"

"I can. The engine is fully operational. I detect a large amount of water in various locations along both port and starboard sides of the ship, but the impact has been minimized by shutting the internal leak containment walls."

"Okay. Then raise them again. I, Pitohui, give you, Clara, a direct order: Raise all leak-containment partitions. No matter what happens, do not prevent the ship from taking on any further water."

Only the humans present were taken aback by this. For her part, Clara simply said, *"Understood. Opening all containment walls. Walls will not be closed until further orders."*

One of the control monitors featured a representation of the ship. The image flickered, and the doors displayed in green turned red. Then the blue area of the diagram began to expand, starting from the outer part of the ship. That was clearly a display of the water level within the craft.

"So it'll follow any order, huh? Even one that sinks itself...," Ervin said, shocked.

"It just means it prioritizes human commands over self-preservation. A very faithful hound," David murmured.

"Are you insane? Why would you sink the dry ground under our feet?" Eva gasped, but Pitohui ignored the question.

"How long will we hold up, Clara?"

"Predictions will change depending on sea conditions, but at the present rate of water intake, I would estimate between two hours and two hours, twenty minutes, until stability is permanently lost."

Pitohui gave Eva a wink. "We're in a death match here. It's not going to take *that* long, is it?"

*   *   *

When Eva had no response, Ervin was the next to speak, at a louder volume than anything he'd produced so far.

"Miss Pitohui! I have a request!"

His full helmet buzzed with faint motor sounds and opened from the jaw upward along hinges at his temples. For the first time, his actual character's face was revealed.

It was the face of a young, skinny man with light-brown skin. He looked earnest and desperate, like he was about to tell someone that he was in love with them.

"What is it?"

"This ship still works, right? Please, pilot it to the northwest!"

"Ah, I see. You want to help out your old teammates who are stuck on the roof of the building over there, right?"

"Yes!"

Eva grunted to herself. David grimaced. They understood the implication of this—and they knew Pitohui did, too.

If the other five members of T-S were unharmed and conveniently able to jump on board the cruise ship, they represented quite a lot of battle power.

It was known that T-S's overall power was not that high, but they had extensive armor that gave them phenomenal defense. And unlike M's shield, they could move and fight wearing their gear. That represented a real danger to the other teams in indoor combat.

But the leader of Team BTRY merely said, "Sure, let's do that." She addressed the ship. "Clara, put us on, heading three-one-five degrees, full speed ahead. There should be a tall building breaching the water, so inform me when we are approaching it."

"Understood. I can perform this order."

"Th-thank you! Thank you so much!" Ervin said, bowing.

The ship swayed a bit. There was a light sensation of moving backward that persisted for some time. It also tipped to the right briefly, then swung broadly to the left. That was evidence that the ship was making a hard right turn.

The other two were silent, but they implied a question about Pitohui's judgment.

"The more the merrier, isn't that what they say?" she asked. It was odd, given that she'd been fighting to lower the numbers just moments ago.

But she was already pushing all of this out of her mind. "All right, what will happen with the scan, now that we're on the ship? Might be time to check this bad boy out."

She pulled the Satellite Scanner from her waist pouch.

✳   ✳   ✳

There are places within the ship displaying a large, lowercase i *mark. By swiping this device near them, you can temporarily access the ship's systems*, said a message on Llenn's Satellite Scanner when she brought it out to check it in the middle of the hallway.

"What does this mean?"

"It'll be obvious when you try it. Like right there, for example," said Fukaziroh, motioning to the side wall no more than fifteen feet away, where that very mark was displayed.

It was just before the corner where another hallway intersected this one—and next to an inactive monitor and broken phone receiver.

The three walked over to it, and Llenn swung her terminal over the mark on the wall. The screen turned on. Llenn set it to holographic display so all three could easily see the result.

It was the same thing that SHINC, MMTM, and the audience were seeing: a map of the ship.

From the lowest passenger cabins on Deck 1 to the uppermost Deck 20, every single floor was shown one by one like tomato slices.

The first five decks had the lower passenger cabins. It was easy to identify them because of the way the rooms were neatly crammed together, with two long hallways that ran the length of the ship. There was a large theater in the fore section of these decks.

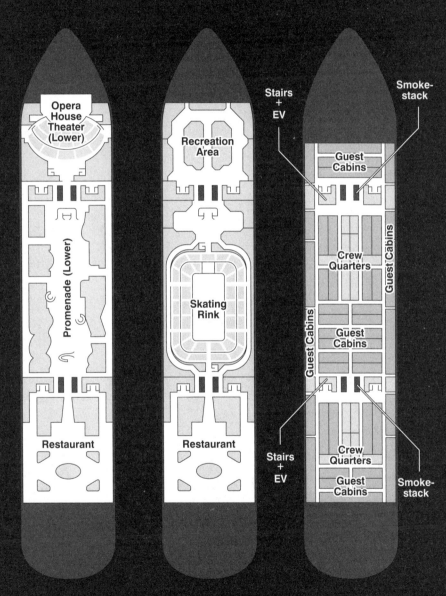

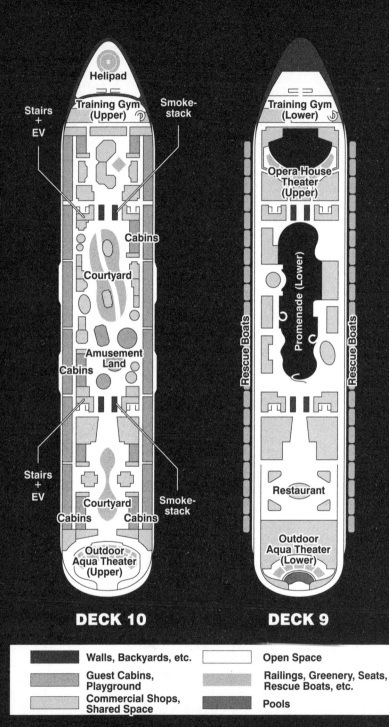

DECK 10

DECK 9

Helipad

Stairs + EV

Training Gym (Upper)

Smoke-stack

Cabins

Courtyard

Amusement Land

Cabins

Stairs + EV

Courtyard

Cabins

Cabins

Smoke-stack

Outdoor Aqua Theater (Upper)

Training Gym (Lower)

Opera House Theater (Upper)

Rescue Boats

Promenade (Lower)

Rescue Boats

Restaurant

Outdoor Aqua Theater (Lower)

	Walls, Backyards, etc.		Open Space
	Guest Cabins, Playground		Railings, Greenery, Seats, Rescue Boats, etc.
	Commercial Shops, Shared Space		Pools

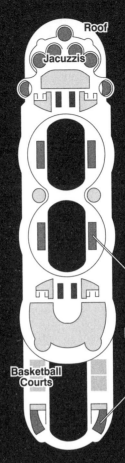

Roof

Jacuzzis

Pools

Basketball
Courts

DECKS 18–19

Roof

Pool

DECK 20

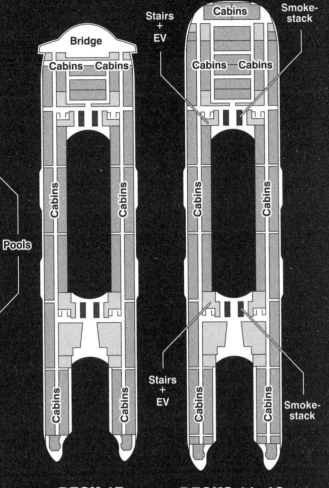

Bridge

Cabins — Cabins

Stairs
+
EV

Cabins

Cabins — Cabins

Smoke-
stack

Cabins

Cabins

Cabins

Cabins

Cabins

Cabins

Stairs
+
EV

Cabins

Cabins

Smoke-
stack

Cabins

Cabins

DECK 17

DECKS 11–16

THE 3rd SQUAD JAM
"THERE IS STILL TIME"
FLOOR MAP

Deck 6 to Deck 9 were non-cabin facilities. There was a spacious entrance hall and enormous restaurants. The smaller interior portions were probably stores. This was where the promenade deck was, too.

Deck 10 had the courtyard deck. From 10 to 16, the cabins were split on the port and starboard sides. In other words, every room had either an ocean view or an interior courtyard view, split by the hallway in between.

Deck 17 appeared to be a multipurpose space split into several large rooms. At the very front was the bridge, the ship's brain.

Above that, Decks 18 to 20 were considered the rooftop, with bridges that spanned the courtyard between the two sides and large, flat areas containing pools, a basketball court, observation decks, and so on.

Since the island was submerged now, there was no need for any other information. This was the new field map.

"Ah, I see. Won't get lost now. Also…"

Llenn pointed at the one dot on the map that was shining.

It was on the bottom deck, all the way at the fore starboard edge.

"That's where we are now, I suppose."

"So this place with the candle symbol is like the index of the ship, huh?" Rosa said.

"It's not a candle, it's a lowercase *i* for *information*," pointed out Anna.

"I don't really get the difference."

"That's all right. At least I can remember the ship map now! It's way simpler than that underground labyrinth!" said Tanya confidently. As the point person, she had a good mind for directions.

"So I guess we can't use the Satellite Scan feature the same way on the ship. How will we locate the enemy in that case?" Kenta wondered.

None of his teammates replied. Instead, the screen of the terminal answered his question.

Scans will happen every five minutes and display all player names and locations for sixty seconds, it read.

"Okay. And it's 1:18 now," Bold announced, reading the time off the screen. "No, wait, 1:19 now."

Then the ship began to move.

Time passed, one second at a time, slowly but surely.

"What is this? Are we moving? Where are we going?" Llenn wondered, feeling the vibration of the ship.

Fukaziroh replied, "Who knows? Doesn't really matter, does it? Where do you want to go, Llenn?"

Her answer was immediate: "Wherever Pito is."

Forty seconds to go.

"As soon as it shows up, we attack the nearest squad! They won't even need to show another scan."

"You bet."

"Got it!"

In the hallway, MMTM was preparing for a charge to wipe out their enemies.

In the lead was Kenta, with his G36K. Behind him to the right was Summon, who had the SCAR-L. They were a team that fired in unison when they attacked, but that meant that if Kenta was careless and moved his upper half, his back and head would get shot. Still, they'd done this many times before.

Behind them was Jake, the present leader of the squad, carrying an HK21 machine gun with a hundred-round ammo box attached.

Bringing up the rear was Bold, of the ARX160. His job was to watch their six and be their backup when they were out of ammo.

Twenty seconds to go.

"Hmm, so that's the deal. Verrry interesting," murmured Pitohui in the bridge as she read the message. "It's kind of too bad," she added.

"Too bad? What do you mean?" Eva asked.

Pitohui waved the device and said, "I don't think any other teams will make it up here within five minutes. We're going to be so bored without any battle."

Ten seconds to go.

The first onboard scan was underway.

It started from above. Scan lines ran through the Deck 20 outline starting from the prow and passing through the stern in the span of a single second.

From there, it scanned each deck separately, going down the ranks. The first positive response came from Deck 17, where the bridge was. It displayed Pitohui and her three companions. The shining dots showed the character's name when touched. Since they were standing in close proximity, the dots were practically overlapping. They did not disappear, even after the scan moved on to lower decks.

"Well, well, first-class seating," Fukaziroh opined lazily.

"Pito's right there! And Eva!" Llenn shouted.

This was the first moment she became aware that Eva, aka Boss, was on Team Betrayers.

What do I do now...? she wondered, question marks flying.

That was her opponent to defeat in SJ3, but she was honestly at a loss for what to do. If she beat Eva when she wasn't with SHINC, did that really count as fulfilling the promise?

But more importantly!

Llenn got her head back in gear and examined the screen again. She had no idea exactly how many players were on the ship at the moment.

Did all the teams get on board safely, the way her team did?

Did they lose one or two along the way?

Did they all get stuck outside the ship and drown in the ocean?

Hopefully, it was the latter.

Then the scan reached Deck 8, and Llenn's hopes were dashed.

It showed the members of MMTM on the aft port side. But

there were only four of them. David, their leader, was on the betrayers' team, so apparently one was gone from SJ3 now.

From that point on, the scan was a total whiff. Nobody showed up. There were six teams approaching the ship, so how could there only be one showing up so far?

At last, the scan reached the bottom, Deck 1.

Llenn and LPFM saw the results.

Rosa and SHINC saw the results.

"Huh?"

"Huh?"

They both squawked at the same time.

LPFM's trio was near the front of the ship, at the end of the long right-hand hallway.

SHINC's quartet was near the front of the ship, at the end of the long left-hand hallway.

And both were standing right before the shorter side hallway that connected both long vertical hallways.

They were no more than fifty yards apart.

"Run! Get beyond that intersection!" M shouted.

"Hya!" "Yo!"

Llenn and Fukaziroh sprang forward.

On the opposite side of the ship, Rosa bellowed and leaped out in front of the side corridor.

"Raaaah!"

Dut-dut-dut-dut-dut-dut-dut-dut-dut-dut-dut-dut-dut-dut-dut!

She blasted her PKM machine gun.

If Llenn and Fukaziroh had been one step slower in leaping across, they would have been caught in Rosa's hail of bullets. Fukaziroh in particular, lacking Llenn's burst, barely made it in time. Two shots hit her bulging backpack, throwing off her balance and causing her to tumble wildly.

If the plasma grenades had still been inside, the chain explosion might have killed them all at once.

"Yeowww!"

Fukaziroh's spill was so violent that her two grenade launchers fell and clattered away. But to their good fortune, they had the ability to flee down toward the aft side of the ship now. Only M, the one who ordered them to do it, was left behind on the fore side. The bullets flew just fifty yards before blasting through the far wall of the hallway. Red bullet lines and the projectiles that followed them carved up the wall. There was no way for M to get past them unharmed.

Rosa lowered the PKM she was firing from her waist to the floor, setting it up on the low bipod so she could lie down behind it.

"Now go!" she yelled as she resumed firing.

"Yeah!" replied Tanya without missing a beat.

While machine-gun bullets hurtled down the side hallway at speeds over Mach 2, Tanya ran alongside them, a few inches away from their path—toward the enemy.

Just from hearing the machine-gun fire pause for an instant, M intuited SHINC's strategy. "Attacker coming!" he bellowed.

Right in front of him, the bullets were coming down the side hallway from the right. Llenn and Fukaziroh were on the other side of them, with the latter being closer to the corner.

"Fuka! Shoot one into the hallway!"

"Hell yeah!"

She grabbed one of the MGL-140s off the ground before her, crawled back toward the hallway the bullets were coming down, and poked the launcher's gaping muzzle around the corner, down low.

"Take this!"

Pomp! She fired once.

A grenade shot from a launcher would not explode on impact if it landed within seventy-five feet of the gun. That was to protect the shooter from the effect of the blast. The method of determining this was simple but effective: The explosive rotated like a bullet as it flew and would not activate unless it crossed a certain number of rotations.

But even if it didn't explode, it was a hunk of metal an inch and a half across, so it could do plenty of damage to a human body just as a physical projectile.

If it was lucky enough to hit the charging attacker—unseen, but almost certainly Tanya—it could probably knock her unconscious.

"Ai-hya!"

The grenade unleashed down the hallway missed Tanya's head by less than an inch. But while it didn't hit *her*...

"Uh-oh, that might be bad," she muttered as she ran.

For having been shot blind, the grenade traveled in a perfect arc down the hallway. It did not hit either of the side walls, but it flew almost exactly straight down the corridor—passing over Rosa's head where she was firing the PKM—and struck the back wall of the port-side hallway.

That was a shot of at least fifty yards.

Naturally, the detonator activated.

The result was a blue explosion.

Rosa, who was lying in the middle of the side hallway, and Anna and Tohma, who were in wait for support whenever she ran out of ammo, all found themselves helpless at the whim of a world of blue.

Their hit points and avatars evaporated into nothingness.

The diameter of the blast was over sixty feet. Tanya was farther than that down the hallway, so she was not affected, but when an explosion happens in an enclosed space, what happens to the surroundings is obvious—it creates a much more focused blast.

The tailwind of the tremendous blast of air shot through the hallway, inescapable, and punched Tanya in the back as though with an air gun.

"Byaaa!"

She traveled through the remaining sixty feet of hallway in the air.

The blast exhaust passed down the side hallway and reached the starboard-side long hallway, where it split in two down either direction.

"Hyaa!" shrieked small, light Llenn, who tumbled over thirty feet backward. Even Fukaziroh, who was slightly heavier, uttered a "Bwoof!" and tumbled back off the floor.

A normal grenade would have been plenty powerful, but Fukaziroh had shot her plasma grenades instead. As she tumbled, she wailed, "Oh nooo! I shot Leftania by mistake!"

"You dummyyyyyyyyyy!" screamed Llenn as she bounced off the walls of the hallway like a Ping-Pong ball.

"Bwuhb!"

Tossed by the explosion, Tanya slammed into the bullet-ridden far wall on the starboard-side hallway, face and stomach first. She flattened there like a frog that had been stepped on.

Her plan to toss a hand grenade as she approached the corner, then leap in behind the blast and fire in both directions, had been accelerated in a most unexpected manner.

The impact cost her quite a lot of HP, but she still had half of her health left. Tanya fell off the wall and landed on her back in the hallway. Very close by, M was crouched to withstand the force of the explosion.

It was clear that her three companions had died instantly, so Tanya leaped up to take revenge against this enemy. "Damn youuuu!"

She'd never let go of the Bizon through all the force of the explosion, and she turned it toward him and tugged on the trigger.

Sh-pang!

One bullet, quieted through the suppressor, hit M's right leg.

Tanya thought, *Huh? I had it on semiauto?*

It was her normal style to always have it on full auto and use the timing of her finger to put together three-to-four-shot bursts.

It seemed that hitting the wall had somehow shifted her Bizon's selector to semiauto.

Well, no problem! Die, M! This is revenge for last time! she thought, placing the bullet circle over M's forehead.

He was only ten feet away. It would take a miracle for her to miss. Even tough-looking M wouldn't survive thirty rounds of 9 mm bullets. She had him.

Tanya pulled the trigger. The hammer clicked. No bullet emerged from the Bizon.

"Eh?"

She looked down at her gun—and finally realized what was missing.

A magazine.

The cylindrical magazine that should be attached to the lower part of the Bizon's front had completely fallen out of the gun. It must have happened when she hit the wall. The only reason she hadn't noticed earlier was that the first time she pulled the trigger, it was able to shoot the single bullet in the chamber.

"Rnng," grunted M, who suffered only a shot to the leg. He looked up, right as Llenn shouted "M!"

Realizing that Llenn was still alive behind her, Tanya acted without hesitation.

She leaped as high as her agility could get, headfirst, barely clearing M as he made to stand up. One of his thick arms reached up to grab her leg, but he wasn't in time.

"Move, M!" cried Llenn, who could no longer shoot at Tanya.

"Hissss!" Tanya twisted like a cat as she landed, turning around to pounce and attack.

She had the Strizh pistol at her side, but she did not use it this time. She already had a weapon that she could use more quickly and effectively within her hands.

Tanya jumped onto M's backpack and used the Bizon's sling, a strip of nylon, to tug on M's neck. Then she rotated the Bizon a full turn, tangling the sling strap, and used all her weight to hang on to it.

"Gfh!"

The inch-wide nylon strap caught on M's throat, and the full weight of the five-foot-five Tanya, still the smallest member of SHINC, dragged him backward.

"Hey! M!"

All Llenn could see, with her P90 at the ready, was M choking and struggling about fifteen yards away. He was so big that she couldn't see Tanya behind him at all. She couldn't shoot.

"Rrrgh…"

M was in pain. He wriggled and writhed, but Tanya clung to the strap behind him like it was a swing, screeching, "I'll never let go, even after death!"

His hands were free from the M14 EBR so he could grab at the sling around his neck. But it was crossed—and so tight that his large fingers couldn't work their way under the material. Still, he scrabbled at the skin so hard that the system calculated he broke through and suffered damage as a result.

"Grugh…"

Ten seconds of thrashing later, M had used up all his oxygen, and his hit points began to dwindle. He was suffocating. At this rate, he was going to die in well under a minute.

"Wh-what should I do?!" Llenn wailed.

"He's obviously saying *Forget me, just shoot!*" observed Fukaziroh rather casually.

"You dummy! I'm only going to hit M!"

"Huh? You mean the bullets won't go through him?"

"They might, but he's got the backpack with the shield inside right behind him!"

"Oh yeah, that's no good. M's guardian spirit has ruined the day. The thing that protects him will be his downfall. Cruel, cruel irony. Really encapsulates the whole tragedy of the human condition in one image."

"Stop acting so nonchalant!"

"Hey, you want me to finish the job, then? That's the only surviving Amazon, right? We could pull back, then I'll shoot six grenades once we're a few dozen yards away. They'll both die."

"You—"

Dummy! Llenn was going to say, but something gave her pause.

Perhaps Fukaziroh's cold, callous strategy had some logic behind it. If M was going to get killed, and Tanya escaped to be a huge hassle with her indoor speed, then maybe it *would* be best to end it here…

"No, we can't do that!" Llenn said, shaking her head. When Llenn, with her outrageously high agility, did this, it looked like her head was creating afterimages, it was moving so fast. If there was a world championship for head-shaking rotation speed, she would wipe out the competition.

Instead, she shouted, "M, you can do it!"

"You can do it, Silver! Choke M out!"

"You got this!"

"Hang in there!"

The audience in the pub cheered and roared at the valiant effort of SHINC's last surviving member. In a world of guns, the method of strangling earned some fanatical excitement from the crowd.

Since the hallway was narrow, the camera had to be close, too. It caught the look of anguish on M's features and fox-faced Tanya gritting her canines with enjoyment, all in close-up.

"…"

M struggled, unable to get any air through his throat. His large body flailed left and right, but he could not throw Tanya off. Then he tried smashing her against the walls of the hallway.

"Daaah!" She was too agile, however. She twisted to avoid contact.

Oh no, M's in trouble… He's in major trouble…

All Llenn could see was huge M struggling. On the left edge of her vision, his hit points were dropping, picking up speed, and were now under a third of their original value.

Then he fell to his knees. He slumped, powerless.

Too late…, Llenn thought, a split second before M jumped up. It was a huge jump, using all his strength. He made contact with the ceiling, back first.

"Gerf!"

Tanya ended up squashed between the ceiling and his backpack. There was enough power in the blow that the ceiling tiles were damaged by it.

"Ooh!" Llenn cheered.

Once M landed, he jumped again.

"*Gahk!*"

He jumped.

"*Gurg!*"

He jumped.

"*Bwuh!*"

At last, Tanya officially took numerical damage from hitting the ceiling. Still, she kept a tight grip and continued choking him, so M fought through his anguish and kept jumping.

"......"

All Llenn could do was watch it happen.

After she had lost track of the number of jumps, Tanya finally screamed an "Aaaah!" and let go. M immediately ripped aside the loosened sling strap.

"Bwaaaah!"

He sucked in a huge breath, and his hit points stopped decreasing. He had about 20 percent of his health left.

Slumped on the carpet, half-alive and half-dead, Tanya muttered "Dammit..." and reached for her waist, grabbing loose a hand grenade and pulling the safety pin.

"Hmph!"

Immediately after, M's thick, horselike leg completely bowled Tanya over backward. She flew several yards down the hallway but kept her grip on the grenade. She tried to throw it but couldn't manage to do more than weakly drop it in front of her.

"Ahhh, shit, it didn't work...," Tanya muttered. Then she vanished into graphical polygon shards and bounced out of SJ3 altogether.

A number of the grenade's shrapnel pieces hit M's leg, causing even more HP damage.

"M! You're all right!"

"Yeah...somehow."

The damage stopped at 10 percent. M had avoided death, and he immediately stuck an emergency healing kit into his hand.

For a brief instant, M's entire form, gear included, shone. That was the beginning of the healing process, which would slowly recover 30 percent of his health over a span of 180 seconds.

From the scan revealing their locations to now, the entire battle took less than two minutes.

"Way to go, M! I knew you would do it!" said Fukaziroh, who moments ago had suggested killing them both to save trouble.

"Ha-ha-ha..." Llenn's laugh was dry. *But at least he survived...*, she thought, truly relieved.

"You know, I was wondering, though," Fukaziroh said, tilting her head to the side. "Why didn't you just turn around, M? Then Llenn could have shot her from behind."

"......"

M's craggy face seemed to hitch a little bit. Llenn chose to speak in his stead.

"Why didn't you say that *earlierrrr*?!"

Her scream came at the same moment the ship silently tilted to the left.

CHAPTER 14
Pitohui's Trap

SECT.14

CHAPTER 14
Pitohui's Trap

The plasma grenade that Fukaziroh accidentally shot off exploded on the ship's port side near the prow, completely obliterating everything within its blast radius.

The guest cabins along the waterside were blown out, the ceiling was blown out—even the lower deck and exterior hull, too.

If someone was hypothetically watching the ship from the outside, they would have seen a blue orb appear first, then debris exploding outward and falling into the sea, then an enormous hole left behind in the side of the ship—as well as a huge volume of seawater flooding into it.

The giant hole appeared over the waterline, and more and more seawater began to spill inside.

While the entire ship might have been 1,600 feet in length, the explosion happened just a few dozen feet below the bridge. The people there certainly felt the vibration and sound of it.

"Ah, that must be SHINC and Llenn's team going at it," Pitohui deduced, putting her Satellite Scan terminal away.

A minute ago, two teams were on the lowest deck and barely separated by any distance, which she'd certainly seen on the map.

"What was that?" Eva asked. "A plasma grenade?"

Pitohui shrugged. "Sorry about all this. I was the one who gave the little grenadier some plasmas this time around, so that's probably what it was."

"……"

Eva said nothing. If such a weapon had been shot at close range immediately following the scan, and it exploded, there was no question what happened to the four in its path.

"They're wiped out," Ervin murmured. The pigtailed woman heard him and closed her eyes.

As a matter of fact, Tanya had escaped the blast and fought hard, nearly taking out M in the process, but Eva couldn't know that from here.

"Whatever happened, we'll find out the details at the next scan. More importantly, now…"

Pitohui switched from speaking to her human partners to speaking to Clara.

"Clara. That punched a big hole in the side of the ship, didn't it? How much water are we taking on?"

"A large amount of water is entering the port side of the Deck 1 area. When the ship begins listing to the left, even more flooding will result. It may mean the ship sinking happens earlier than the previous estimate."

"Ah, how scary," said Pitohui in a tone that contained no fear whatsoever.

"Please, do not be frightened," said Clara automatically. The computer could not process subtler emotions.

Then the ship began to lean to the left. The angle was sharper than when it was turning. It was clear from the shift that this was an abnormal state of affairs.

"Shall I take in more water to starboard, in order to balance out the ship? It will result in a greater amount of flooding overall," Clara asked.

"……"

Pitohui did not give her an immediate answer. She looked at her watch. It was 1:23, two minutes from the next scan.

Twenty seconds passed in silence. Eventually, David broke the silence to ask, "Hey, what's the holdup?"

"Level us out for now, Clara," said Pitohui. "Then stop when it gets to one thirty."

"Understood. I will endeavor to even out the ship by one thirty."

It was an odd order, but the computer gamely accepted the challenge, to the skeptical looks of David, Eva, and Ervin.

"What are you thinking?" Boss asked.

Pitohui just showed her palm, an indication that she would explain later. Then she continued, "Clara, show me the wiring layout of the ship. And the location of the sprinklers."

That only further confused the other three. A ship diagram appeared on one of the control monitors.

"What's going on?"

MMTM had no idea about the explosion or the increased flooding.

"Feels like we've been listing to the side for a bit… This isn't a turn, is it?"

Kenta and Summon were in the lead position, but now they stopped. Naturally, so did Jake behind them and Bold in the rear.

The four were in the left hallway of Deck 10. That was the floor with the courtyard. They were walking past guest cabins at the moment, but if needed, they could cross through one of the interior-side rooms to get out into the courtyard at any moment.

They were heading for the bridge, of course. To defeat the team of betrayers.

The thought of battle ahead was tantalizing for them all, but Kenta summed up their mood by saying, "There's no point to this if the ship sinks first…"

MMTM stopped for a minute or so, hoping to figure out what was happening to the ship.

"Oh, it's going back," Kenta observed. It was slowly tilting to the right, regaining its balance.

Bold said, "That was nerve-racking... It would be terrible if we finally reached the safety of the ship, only to have it sink on us."

"*Could* you sink this ship, if you intended to? I just assumed that once it started floating, it would be stable until the event was over. Am I wrong about that?" Lux wondered.

It was the present team leader, Jake, who answered, "It's possible... Remember, you can destroy a whole lot of stuff in *GGO*...including every possible vehicle you can ride. So this ship probably isn't an exception. And that madwoman is on the bridge, too. There's no telling what she might try to do..."

Jake shivered, remembering being skewered through the eye last time. Worried, he said, "Which is easier for handling the tilt, the interior hallways or a more open space?"

"I don't know. Obviously, I don't mind interior combat, but I don't like my feet being unsteady," said Kenta.

"The benefit of a tighter area is that we can lean on the walls... but even that's not ideal," said Summon.

"So the open areas are where we can actually make use of our firepower," said Bold.

Jake the leader was silent for five seconds.

"......"

He checked his wristwatch. The time was exactly 1:24. One minute until the next scan. No, fifty-nine seconds. Fifty-eight. Fifty-seven...

"We're going into the courtyard! Then we'll wait for the scan."

Considering how MMTM always charged their way through things, it seemed like a passive, weak strategy. If David were still the team leader, he would not have made such a choice.

"Got it."

"Roger."

"Might as well play it safe."

But the other three members had no objections, so away they went.

*   *   *

MMTM traveled to the end of the hallway leading to the court-yard, waiting for 1:25 to arrive. Jake crouched before the wall with the *i* symbol, with the others arranged around him at intervals of a few yards.

"It's so wide open... Makes you forget you're actually in the middle of a ship...," Kenta marveled, poking his head around the corner.

The courtyard ran about 1,100 feet long and 160 feet wide, bordered by two huge structures on either side. It could be considered a massive shopping street.

On the sides were a number of stores, just like any outdoor shopping mall. Some of the places were commercial shops, others were restaurants and cafés. It was all ruined now, of course, but it was still in pristine enough condition that Squad Jam participants could immediately see what it would have been like originally. It was "decorated" to suggest that the refugees had lived there, with mattresses, blankets, and clothes strewn inside and outside the stores.

In the center and down the sides of the courtyard were paved pathways wide enough for a car to drive down. They were almost surely not using real stone, but some kind of lightweight tile.

On the sides of the central path were planters and trees for the passersby to enjoy. It gave the place a parklike feel. The plants had dried up and died, and there were signs that the planters had been dug up and used as impromptu fields. Perhaps they planted potatoes. The occasional bench in the area was rusted over.

Around the middle of the courtyard, directly in the center of the ship as a whole, was an amusement park area. It had a merry-go-round, spinning teacups, and a rotating swing ride. There was even one of those swinging Viking ship rides, which was odd, considering it was already on a giant ship.

The courtyard was open on top, meaning it was susceptible to rain. Everything exposed to the elements had more rust than elsewhere, around the stores and attractions.

Nothing had power out here. Either the electricity was dead or the lines had been cut off long ago. But given the light coming down from the reddish-gray sky, there wasn't much need for illumination.

The bridge, where they would find the betrayers, was above and beyond the prow end of the courtyard. How MMTM acted next would depend greatly on the location of the enemy team.

If members of BTRY were blockading themselves in the bridge, that would be a stroke of good fortune. They could pass right through the courtyard without worrying about a fight, race up the stairs at the front of the ship, then, at the bridge, they could engage in interior combat, their forte as a team. They'd simply have to be on the lookout for ambushes or traps.

If BTRY split up and hid elsewhere around the ship to fight back, however, that would also be a welcome development. In that case, MMTM would speedily approach and attack, maintaining firepower supremacy, and finish them off one by one. That would be similar to what they did to the team inside the spaceship in SJ1.

Of course, given that their former leader, David, was among BTRY now, he would be aware of that strategy.

If Pitohui the madwoman was among them, she was almost certainly going to have some strategy that would be both effective and completely unexpected. Something that would eliminate their strength: good interior combat skill and effective teamwork.

"So what are they gonna do...?" Jake wondered, four parts worry to one part anticipation, right as the scan started.

The earlier scan started from the upper decks, but this one began from the lowest. It seemed it was going to change for each scan.

Jake had his companions watch the ends of the hallway while he viewed the scan for the rest of the team.

There was no one on Decks 1 or 2.

On Deck 3, three members of LPFM were near the prow. It was about the same location as the earlier scan, only two decks higher. It seemed as though they'd simply climbed the stairs. If they weren't being aggressive, it probably meant they were taking their time and healing up.

"Pink shrimp's team is still on the third floor, fore. Recovering? Just watch out for her, since she moves faster than a human being can. The women aren't on the same deck as them. Highly likely they've been wiped out," Jake reported, covering the details quickly. He waited for more information as the scan rose through the ship.

Despite being one second per floor, it felt slower. He waited, praying for Deck 10 to come sooner.

On the left side, adjacent to the courtyard near the stern, it displayed their locations accurately. Since SHINC hadn't appeared on any of the floors up to this point, his suspicion that they were eliminated turned to certainty.

It also told him that none of the BTRY members were on the same floor—and that they knew where MMTM was now. He tensed, waiting for David to launch a grenade from a higher deck, but there was no incoming attack.

Did that mean they weren't nearby?

"Amazons are definitely out. No Team Betrayers on this floor. Waiting for higher scans," said Jake as his teammates waited with nerves taut. The three had their fingers on the triggers of their rifles.

The scan continued upward. Decks 11, 12, 13, and 14 passed without any results.

"Nothing up to Fourteen yet…"

Next it passed through Decks 15 and 16.

"Still nothing at Sixteen…"

Were they hanging out on the bridge? A team with both David and Pitohui—hanging out? The question marks floated over Jake's head.

Next was Deck 17.

"What the—?! They're all still on the bridge!" he said, stunned.

The Satellite Scanner showed that all four members of Team BTRY were clustered at the edge of the ship's bridge. In other words, there were no humans capable of attacking them anytime soon.

"Okay! Courtyard is clear! Everyone, run!"

"Got it!" "Uh-huh!" "Okay!"

Freed from the tension of the moment, the other three happily responded, and MMTM rushed out into the courtyard.

Even after the scan had finished with each floor, the player's location would remain displayed for the next sixty seconds. On Pitohui's device, she saw the dots with the names of Jake, Bold, Kenta, and Summon rush into the open area.

Whether a sign of confidence or a message that they were coming, they showed no intention of hiding what they were doing.

And when she saw them heading toward the fore of the ship, Pitohui gave an order: "Activate."

"They're going!"

"Yes! Wipe 'em out!" yelled the audience when they saw MMTM charge.

"Oh?" They also spotted something before anyone else did. "Is that rain?"

Droplets were running across the screen at a diagonal angle. There were only a few at first, but then they increased in number until it quickly became a furious shower.

"Huh? Is it raining?" Kenta wondered, noticing the storm of droplets as he ran straight toward the group. He looked up and saw water falling through the space between the sides of the ship, and within moments, his face was drenched.

The large droplets splattered against his face and naturally went down into his mouth.

"Gah! It's salty!" He grimaced.

"What is this? Is it seawater instead of rain?" Summon wondered. The natural rain in *GGO* clearly had something weird dissolved into it, but it had never been as obviously salty as this. At first glance—er, taste—it was clearly seawater.

As he ran, Jake gasped, "Why is seawater falling from the sky…?"

"You don't think the sea's risen all the way up to the top of the buildings to the sides?" Bold asked preposterously. If that were true, the fore and aft sections of the ship would have been submerged long ago.

"Wait, that's not rain. That's a sprinkler," Kenta observed, pointing out a spot on the ceiling. From over the edge of the balcony of one of the interior cabins ran a small hose that was gushing out water.

From there, it was unclear how many hoses were producing water. They seemed to exist on each deck going up, so there were far more than just ten or twenty.

All the makeshift sprinklers combined to emit a tremendous amount of seawater. This artificial rain soaked the cobblestones of the courtyard in moments, creating puddles. The spray of the hoses and the splashing upon impact decreased visibility so that their goal, the fore end of the courtyard, was no longer visible.

There was still five hundred feet to go. They'd crossed a little more than half of the open area.

"This is a mess," Kenta muttered as he raced through the spray.

Behind him, Summon was more optimistic. "But it's not actually damaging us, and it makes it harder for them to see us, right? What's the harm?"

True, even if BTRY suddenly came down to attack, there was much less worry about a possible sniper.

So MMTM rushed through the buckets of water pelting them and approached the amusement park area. Only three hundred feet to their destination now.

In less than a minute, the courtyard was completely soaked. And either the drainage system of the courtyard was weak to begin with or the pump wasn't working at all, because the rain didn't wash away—just piled up higher and higher.

They kicked up water as they ran, the liquid reaching the top of their boots now. They were completely soaked, but no one was concerned about that.

Their guns were waterlogged, but good military hardware wasn't going to malfunction from a little adverse weather. Even after being submerged in water for a little while, the gunpowder in the cartridges would still ignite, so players could even shoot them underwater if they really wanted. They just wouldn't shoot very far.

If anything, in rain or spray like this, optical guns would suffer the biggest loss of power. That didn't matter here, because nobody had one.

"We can do this! If we fight them indoors, we've got a chance to win!" said Jake, the leader. He smiled, and some seawater got into his mouth. "Bleh, that's salty!"

At that moment, Kenta was in the lead, passing the side of the merry-go-round. Summon was right at his side, a step behind. Jake was next to the teacups. Lastly, Bold was running past the Viking ship.

"I'm sure. Turn it on," Pitohui commanded at the bridge.
An instant later, all four members of MMTM were dead.

All at once, their bodies seized up.

Their arms and legs went as stiff as if they were tied down. The guns fell from their hands and dangled from the slings around their necks and shoulders.

The men were as stiff as boards, and their entire bodies glowed red with the light that indicated damage suffered. The momentum of their running carried them forward, however, smashing face-first into the puddles on the ground and leaving them face-down under the layer of water that had built up.

Not one of them budged, and within a few seconds, the marker reading DEAD had appeared over each of them.

On the monitors, the four suddenly flashed red, fell over, and were instantly ruled dead. The number four appeared on the side of the screen indicating fatalities, and not a single one of the audience could understand what had just happened.

"Wh-what was that?"

"What the fuh...?"

"Uhhh?"

While the rain made it hard to see, the image of the men running had been quite clear. The crowd could tell that they hadn't been shot or hit by a grenade explosion.

For one thing, the only team that would have attacked them, Pitohui's Betrayers, were still on the bridge. On another monitor, Pitohui stood before the bridge's console, while Ervin, Eva, and David pointed guns toward the room's entrance in case of an enemy invasion. Naturally, there were many walls between this place and the courtyard.

So was it the other surviving team, Llenn's squad? That was also impossible. The trio was still huddling in the Deck 3 hallway, waiting for M to recover from his serious injuries.

So who had killed MMTM, and how?

"I think that probably did the trick. You can stop now, Clara," Pitohui said, who of course knew how they had died—because she was responsible. "But we can't be sure, so will you go and check? Three of you, just in case. When the next scan comes, all three of you check it. I don't think they'll be coming up yet, but be very careful of Llenn making a charge at us," she told her teammates at the entrance to the bridge.

David looked conflicted, Eva was as stoic and stern as ever, and Ervin's face was hidden, but they said, "Got it."

"All right."

"Let's go..."

And left the bridge together at 1:27.

Once her companions exited the bridge along with the marker signifying the presence of a camera, Pitohui was left all alone.

"Ugh..."

She collapsed on the spot and landed faceup next to the magnificent captain's chair.

"What's the matter? Do you feel sick?" asked Clara.

Pitohui removed the comm unit from her ear for a moment and said, "Ugh, I feel sluggish."

"That is not ideal. Are you ill?"

"No, my brain's fried; that's all. It's not firing on all cylinders. If I was using the AmuSphere, it'd be logging me out automatically by now... But all hail the NerveGear... It's a good thing I kept it around..."

"Why do you feel so tired? Is there anything I can do for you? Shall I call the ship doctor?"

"The reason is simple: I worked too much yesterday. The day after a performance, my body always gives out. So there's nothing you can do about that, Clara. Oh, but there are plenty of other things you can do. No worries there."

"I understand. Please give me any orders you wish completed."

1:29 PM.

"Yep, they're all dead...," Eva muttered, looking down on the courtyard of Deck 15 through her Vintorez's scope.

A few yards away, David had a similar bead on the scene with his STM-556. He could count the four DEAD tags over his former squadmates.

The sprinklers had stopped now. The bodies were lying facedown in the shallow amount of seawater flooding the courtyard area.

"She really beat them from the bridge... Incredible... You did it, Pitohui! Brilliant work!" reported Ervin, his voice thick with wonder. He had seen and heard what Pitohui did in person.

A few minutes earlier, when Pitohui learned that MMTM was rushing into the courtyard, she gave Clara two simple orders.

First, to activate the ship's entire sprinkler system at maximum output. Despite the absolute absence of fire onboard, Clara faithfully carried out the command, activating every last internal water spray, tens of thousands of them in all.

Normally, the sprinkler system would use normal water stored in the ship's tanks, but that wasn't very much fluid in the long run. Whatever was left, it was quickly depleted, and so it turned to whatever other water was at hand. In this case, seawater.

Next, Pitohui gave Clara the second order: Activate all power to the courtyard.

There was an amusement park in the courtyard. It featured a number of attractions that ran on electric motor power. Since it involved moving heavy objects very quickly, that meant a considerable voltage and current.

"Are you sure? It is possible that any humans in the area will be fatally electrocuted," Clara asked for confirmation, but Pitohui's answer was brief.

"I'm sure. Turn it on."

$$* \qquad * \qquad *$$

The scan at 1:30 began from the top.

Eva wore an austere look as she muttered, "Only Llenn's team is left, then…"

Ten seconds later, a soaked Llenn watched the scan reach her on Deck 3 and sternly muttered, "Only our team is left, then…"

"LPFM are still down below, so we're safe for a while, right? I'll go look outside!" said Ervin, turning on his heel.

He ran off with the XM8 over his back. On and on he ran, through a totally empty cruise ship.

On the walls as the sci-fi soldier ran past, English messages were scrawled such as *We won't give up!* and *We will survive!* and *The Adam and Eve of a new world!* and *Earth is beautiful* and *We won't repeat their mistakes.*

Ervin raced back up two flights of stairs, returning to Deck 17, which contained the bridge. He sprang through a heavy door on the starboard side and emerged onto a spacious observation deck along the side of the bridge.

Beyond the handrails was a vast gray ocean.

"……"

Ervin clenched the railing with superhuman force and looked along the horizon. The sea was much different now. It was fierce and choppy, not at all the peaceful surface it had been before. Large waves were forming. But because the ship was so huge, he hardly felt any rocking.

If they were heading toward the building, he couldn't tell where it was. Ervin looked from the right edge of the horizon all the way to the left.

"Ah…"

He found it. A tiny little three-story section of a skyscraper was sticking out of the gray desert that was the ocean. It was in the direction the ship was heading, visible directly to the right of the prow.

The distance between the two was maybe nine hundred yards.

"Ah!"

With his helmet's zooming function, he saw them: his friends. All five of them, still on the roof, watching the approaching ship. Some were even waving.

"Pitohui! I see them! They're all alive and well! Thank you! Thank you!" Ervin cried, full of gratitude for the savior who kept his friends in the game.

They had to figure out how the other team was going to jump onto the ship, and once they did, it was unclear how they were going to square up everything before the fighting resumed.

But the mere thought that his squadmates, once thought lost, were still alive with a chance in SJ3 made Ervin jump for joy atop the deck.

"Yes! Yes! Yessss!"

All the while, the ship was getting closer and closer to the building. It wasn't possible to tell what the actual speed was, but it was significant. Full speed, one might say.

In a few dozen seconds, the gap between them went from significant to small. Ervin didn't know much about how ships worked, but he knew that if they didn't put on the brakes soon, they were going to pass the building.

"Miss Pitohui, please stop the ship," he said, but he got no response. "Miss Pitohui?"

He waited a few seconds, but there was still no reply.

"What's the matter?" said David with some concern, his voice traveling to Ervin's ear through the comm earpiece.

"It's just that she's not—," Ervin said, stopping mid-sentence.

The ship was listing a bit to the left. Meaning that it was turning right.

"Huh……?"

It stopped turning when the prow was pointed directly at the approaching building.

The five remaining members of T-S celebrated wildly when they saw the enormous cruise ship heading toward them.

"Yahoooo!"

"They're coming this way!"

"We're saved!"

"So *that's* what was in the middle of the island!"

"Ervin pulled through, boys!"

The armored men numbered 001 through 006 (except for 002) danced and jumped with glee. No longer was there a silent, funereal mood over the rooftop.

The silently rising sea level had been more terrifying than any monster. When it reached four floors beneath their position, they thought they were done for. Some even considered resigning from SJ3, as an alternative to staying put and drowning.

Then, when it finally stopped rising altogether just three stories down, drowning was no longer a concern. They stared dully up at the sky, enviously imagining the battles happening elsewhere. They even wondered about the faint possibility that the last two teams would knock each other out, leaving them as the winners again by default.

Now the ship was as big as a mountain.

The enormous craft, at a speed unbefitting of its size, headed toward them.

And on it came.

And on it came.

"Huh?"

"Oh?"

"What?"

And it plunged.

And it plunged.

"Wh-what the—?"

"Run away!"

"Run *where*?"

And it plunged into them.

From atop the ship, Ervin watched.

From the sky above, the audience watched.

And from the building itself, T-S watched.

…As the titanic cruise ship slammed into the building at full speed.

First, the bulbous bow that extended under the water beneath the prow embedded itself into the side of the building below the waterline. Next, the prow that kicked up waves slammed into the building wall. The sheer kinetic energy of the ship and its momentum was far more than the skinny building could absorb; the prow merely crumpled a tiny bit as it tore through concrete layers.

"Hyaaa!"

"Aieee!"

"Whyyy?"

"Bwaaa!"

The rooftop of the building crumbled beneath T-S's feet, split into two halves by the prow of the ship. The five survivors were tossed into the ashen sea along with all the concrete and rebar, where they sank.

*   *   *

To the audience watching on the monitors in the bar, it looked like a small amount of trash got knocked off the top of the building when it was smashed, but it was clear to them that those were actually people.

"Eep..."

"Yikes..."

"I guess that's one way to kill an opponent..."

"What the hell just happened?"

"I know why this happened. It was Pitohui," they said.

Ervin watched it happen as he screamed, "Miss Pitohui! Stop the boat! Please stop the boat!"

The building where he'd been minutes ago, and where his friends still were, flattened and crumbled like a cracker.

The massive ship lost not a bit of its speed as it smashed through the part of the building above the waterline, as well as what was below it. There was a tiny vibration through his hands and feet from the impact.

"Aaah! Aaah! Aaah! Aaah! Aaah! Aaah!"

All Ervin could do was scream.

It all happened in the span of seconds. The building that had been below him was gone. Nothing floated to the surface. Gray sea and waves were all there was.

"......"

Ervin started running—straight for the nearby bridge of the ship.

"Miss Pitohui!" Ervin cried as he raced into the bridge room, where he saw that things looked pretty much exactly the same.

"Huh?"

Except for Pitohui, collapsed faceup next to the captain's chair. Her KTR-09 was lying on the floor next to her body. Her right hand was reaching for it to no avail, and her left hand was underneath her midriff.

"Huh?"

For a moment, Ervin's mind went blank. He reached her side, crouched, and very carefully shook the shoulder of her navy-blue bodysuit.

"Huh? Um…excuse me?"

There was no response. He gave it a little more force, but still she did nothing.

But there was no DEAD tag over her body, so that meant she had to be alive. According to the hit point bar on the left side of his vision, Pitohui still had full health.

"What is it? What happened? What was that vibration from?" Eva's voice said into his ear.

"The ship…hit the building… Everyone died… Pitohui's collapsed on the bridge…not responding…but not dead…"

"Huh?!" Eva squawked.

"What is this? What's happening right now? What's going on?" Ervin chattered, going into a panic.

David's voice snapped him to attention. "Ervin! Get away from that crazy bitch!"

Ervin couldn't deliver a response to that. A glowing blue beam was penetrating from the chin of his helmet to the back of his head.

The shining rod was connected to a silver tube. And the silver tube was in the left hand within that navy bodysuit.

Pitohui had delivered a surprise lightsword thrust from a prone position on the floor.

"……"

Ervin froze in place, his expression unknown behind the helmet. His shoulders slumped forward, and he silently perished.

"There we go!"

She stashed the lightsword away and leaped backward to get to her feet.

Ervin's armored body thudded chest first against the ground. The DEAD tag pinged into life over him.

Pitohui touched her left ear to turn off the comm item and muttered, "Good grief, why does Daveed have to have such good instincts? I wanted to have more fun with that."

She spun around and proceeded to the console. "Clara, that was a lovely collision! Good job!"

"I'm honored to receive your thanks. I merely carried out the orders I was given," Clara replied just as the clock hit 1:35.

David examined his terminal on Deck 15. "Damn you, Pitohui… You killed Ervin, didn't you…?"

His suspicion became certainty. It was clear from the team's HP bars that Ervin was dead. Where and how he died wasn't exactly clear—but when the scan started at the top deck and quickly showed that Pitohui was alone on the bridge, he discarded the very faint possibility that Llenn had snuck up there, silently knocked out Pitohui, then killed Ervin when he showed up.

Llenn's trio was still all the way down on Deck 7. There were currently only six survivors, including him, Pitohui, and Eva.

Through the comm, Pitohui said, "What? I only sent him to join the friends who sank under the water."

It almost sounded like she expected to be thanked for it.

David didn't bother to hide his loathing. "Keh! And it was on your orders that the ship smashed into that building!"

"I'm affronted that without any evidence you'd treat me like a criminal. Although, it is true. I defeated our enemies, and I don't deserve to be criticized for it. At least I gave Ervin a nice little nugget of hope. He thought he was going to be able to save his buddies. He should thank me for giving him that hope. Just think of how *considerate* I am!"

"Pitohui…I knew that you were a completely irredeemable piece of shit, but I thought you at least took the game seriously.

It's one thing to beat your enemies. But involuntary arrangement or not, I didn't think you'd plot to kill your own teammates. I've lost any respect I had for you."

"Why, don't you dare flatter me. In fact, didn't you watch the entire tape of the last game?"

"I'll say one final thing, though."

"What? That you love me?"

"You are now our enemy," David said, placing his hand to his ear and switching off his communication device. He had nothing left to say to her.

His green-camo-painted face was steaming with righteous anger and the will to fight. He turned to Eva and said, "You do it, too. First things first, we get rid of Pitohui."

Eva raised her hand to her ear, too, but then said, "I understand how you feel, but I'll pass."

"What?"

"I want to fight Llenn. I want to put everything I have into it."

"……"

"But if you want to kill our teammate, I won't shoot you in the back. Now go on and do what you're going to do."

"……I don't know if I should be thanking you or not…"

And with that, David spun around, exposing his back to Eva, and took off running.

His STM-556 was at the ready in front of him, and he left the deck behind to go back into the ship interior, heading for the bridge.

Eva watched him go in silence.

CHAPTER 15

Turn Over

SECT.15

CHAPTER 15
Turn Over

A drenched Llenn stood next to the staircase on the starboard side's
long vertical hallway of Deck 5, watching the 1:35 scan go by.

"What? Why? What in the world happened up there? A betrayer
is gone!" she shouted in disbelief.

Fukaziroh, also drenched, and with her MGL-140s in each
hand, suggested, "Maybe Pito killed them?"

"That's crazy," Llenn said without thinking.

But M, who was recovering hit points beside Fukaziroh,
refuted, "No, I wouldn't put it past her."

For one thing, near the conclusion of SJ2, M had died because
Pitohui was furious that he'd sided with Llen, even slightly, and
shot him.

"If we let it happen, Pito herself could completely demolish the
rest of the betrayers' team."

"That sounds great, M. Should we chill out here for a bit longer?" Fukaziroh said, half-joking and half-serious.

"It's not a bad idea, but it's not going to be an option. The
water's rising again," M noted, glancing down the staircase.

"Already?" Llenn looked down the staircase they'd come up
and saw that the level of the seawater was slowly approaching,
evidence that the ship was taking on more and more water. The
submerged lights farther down were still visible, wavering eerily
through the cloudy churn of water.

Until this point, they'd been taking a strategy of delaying going up to the next floor as long as possible. If they came across an enemy team, they agreed to run and hide, avoiding battle as best they could.

There were two reasons for this.

One was to wait for M's HP to recover. He'd lost nearly all of it in the battle against Tanya, so to get it back to full, they would need all three of his emergency med kits and nine full minutes. That was a vast amount of time in Squad Jam, and it was difficult to go that long without any fighting whatsoever.

The other reason was to get their rivals MMTM to fight Team Betrayers instead. If MMTM came after LPFM, they would be in big trouble.

In total honesty, if they determined that not everyone could escape, M would set up his shield in the hallway and stay behind as a sacrifice. They even considered having Fukaziroh hurl plasma grenades from behind to destroy both M and the enemy together.

Fortunately, however, MMTM chose to fight the betrayers instead. Whatever exactly happened wasn't clear, except that the four completely vanished five minutes before.

All they knew was that the punctured ship continued to sink as water flooded on board. One of the biggest holes being their own responsibility, of course.

First the water rose toward Deck 3, so they moved up to the fourth. When it threatened Deck 4, the trio had no choice but to climb to Deck 5. Llenn took the lead up the stairs, P90 in hand.

"Is this ship really safe, taking on so much water...? Are we gonna sink?" she wondered.

"No idea," said M.

"Damn that bitch!" David swore, loudly because he'd turned off his earpiece, as he ran up the stairs.

They were stairs with spacious landings, where passengers might have greeted one another with smiles when this had been a luxury cruise ship. But now they were faded and filthy, with countless rags draped over the handrails—perhaps someone's ancient clothes.

At the top of the stairs, the open space of Deck 17 came into view, with the door leading to the bridge up ahead. He sprinted the rest of the way, the STM-556 with grenade launcher propped against his shoulder. If he saw anything moving, he was going to view it as a target and pull the trigger.

But strangely enough, David was certain: Pitohui would not make any attempts at him along the way.

She was waiting for him in her lair, the bridge.

"I'm coming for you, demon lord!"

As Pitohui had done when she first came in, David kicked open the door to the bridge. It was a method only someone certain there would be no hand grenade booby traps would use. Indeed, there were no traps.

"Here I am!" he announced.

Naturally, he had his gun at the ready the whole time. If he saw any movement, he was going to open fire on it.

"......"

But there was nothing moving on the ship's bridge.

David had the entire space in view, about the size of a classroom, but there was no one present.

About ten feet ahead on the right side was a sci-fi soldier in armor and helmet, lying facedown and utterly still. An XM8 assault rifle was on the floor beside him.

The console was in the center of the bridge, but there wasn't enough room for a person to hide behind it.

David's eyes moved swiftly—and then he spotted it.

A break in the thick glass of the previously intact windows. In the farthest window to the left, there was a hole barely large enough for a person to squeeze through. The wind moaned softly as it traveled through the hole.

Just two seconds had passed since David barged into the room.

"Shit!"

Pitohui had gotten away. But then he noticed something else wrong in the room.

Something that should have been there was missing.

David turned his gun toward it, and it rose to grab that gun at exactly the same time.

"Ervin" squeezed the barrel of the STM-556 with both hands and yanked with total weight and strength—while making sure the muzzle was pointed away, to prevent being shot.

Rather than trying to hold on and being yanked along and losing his balance, David chose to give up the gun. He let go and reached for his holster with his free right hand to grab the M9-A1 pistol there.

"Die, Pitohui!"

He opened fire on the armored person who was throwing his assault rifle across the room.

A series of shots echoed across the bridge, and fourteen empty cartridges flew into the air—but the person in the armor did not fall.

All the 9 mm pistol rounds bounced off the breastplate and helmet of the suit of armor.

"Dammit!"

The slide stayed back on the M9-A1, and then the armored person took one big stride forward and smacked the pistol with an open-hand slap, knocking it all the way to the corner of the room.

David leaped back to three paces away, and he and the armored player stared at each other.

"So first you kill him, then you steal his gear?! Have you sunk to petty thievery now?!" David shouted, derision clear in his voice and expression. The armored player's left arm waved a little bit, and the armor came off.

The armor broke free and fell away, starting with the limbs, then the chest and the back. The full helmet pulled back from the face first, then rolled entirely off the back of the player's head.

It all clattered dully on the floor of the bridge, revealing the person inside: a woman in a skintight navy-blue bodysuit, with no weapons or items whatsoever, and geometrical-patterned tattoos on her cheeks.

She was smiling.

"Ah, I see your point. Stealing the equipment of the dead is bad. But those it might happen to in this situation are asking for something like this to happen, aren't they? I'm sure Ervin will understand," Pitohui said happily.

David smirked back. "You won't blame me, then, when I kill you? Because I'm the kind of guy who feels like he needs to do that to make it up to his team."

"Aren't you supposed to say you'd rather *starve* than do what I did? Come on, you've got to stick to the script."

"How long are you going to keep this up...?"

"Don't be such a downer, Daveed! Remember, the next scene is where you rip off my clothes and run away yelling 'Hya-hooo!'"

"I'm not doing that! The audience will think I'm a pervert!"

The audience in question had been watching since before David rushed into the bridge room, so they knew who the "Ervin" without a DEAD marker really was.

As they watched him rush to the bridge with murder on his mind, they wondered, "Why is he trying to kill Pitohui?"

"Because she killed their teammate, the armor guy?"

"I don't know why she did that, either... Though I get why she obliterated T-S..."

Then they watched, breathless, as David barged onto the bridge, and Pitohui—in the guise of Ervin's body—leaped up and yanked away his assault rifle, defended against his pistol shots, and they reached a momentary cease-fire.

"Check this out. A quiet stare down before the storm..."

"What are they saying to each other? You'd think they could at least pipe in the mic audio at a moment like this."

"They must be trading some super-badass lines…"

But none of the people watching had any idea that, in fact, they were largely joking about references to Akutagawa Ryūnosuke's short story *Rashōmon*.

"It's time for me to kill you, bandit woman."

On the bridge, David's arm moved smoothly. He reached for the weapon in his waist pouch that had previously been cutting down the wires holding up the rescue boats—his trusty lightsword.

It was a black-handled photon sword that was sold at the store under the name *Nosada N2*.

There were rules for the names of lightswords. First, it had a name taken from a traditional katana, which identified its general design and function. The letter after that indicated the length of the blade, with *A* being the shortest and *Z* the longest. Lastly, the number at the end corresponded to its color.

"Huh? You aren't going to ask *why* I killed Ervin?" Pitohui teased, reaching into the one large pouch on her suit, around the back. She pulled out her own lightsword, the Muramasa F9.

"Why would I expect a reasonable answer? It'll probably be some reason like, 'Because the sun was so bright.'"

"No, it's not something as literary and abstract as that. Ugh, I'm going to have to spell it out, aren't I? Fine, it's the souvenir you can take to the grave with you."

Then she spun the dial on the handle with her thumb to extend the glowing blade outward.

"You see…"

The audience in the pub saw David look momentarily stunned, then break out into a childlike smile of delight. He extended his own red blade.

"What do you suppose she told him?"

*   *   *

"That was the perfect thing to hear at the end! Now you can die without regrets!"

David moved first. He closed the gap, swinging from the right side. The red blade moved so fast that it seemed to smear in the air.

"Hya!"

Pitohui moved her right arm out to the left, then added her other hand for extra strength, shielding against the strike with her own blade.

Bshak! The blades made a bursting sound as they collided, spraying little motes of light.

These lightswords—officially called photon swords in-game—were more of a novelty inserted into *GGO* by one of its designers than a serious weapon.

The designer figured *If you're going to create a sci-fi future world, why not throw in those famous weapons from the legendary movies about stellar warfare? You think swords are weird in a world of guns? Not my problem, pal.*

So while the names and designs were different—at least, just different enough not to be actionable in court—the way they worked was essentially identical.

So like real swords, and like in the movies, the lightswords clashed and smashed like physical objects, meaning fighters could get into a deadlocked pushing match with them.

Pitohui blocked David's blow and used the full strength of both her arms to keep him from overpowering her. Skillfully, she rearranged her feet so she could dart backward, quickly moving across the wide-open bridge. She lifted the lightsword up to a direct stance before her.

"Whew! Very fast. And your swing is pristine and focused. You must have practiced quite a lot, eh?" she gushed.

The lightsword's weight was entirely in the handle alone, so the wielder didn't *feel* like they were holding a three-foot blade. It could be dangerous; if they were careless, they might swing it and cut things around them—or even themselves.

Swinging an object that light around, quickly and directly, required more practice than a gun did. Unlike the sword-centric VR games, this one had no system assistance to help the player swing.

David let his arm fall so the tip of the sword dyed the carpet red, and he smiled. His handsome, camo-painted features were twisted a bit, his right eye open wider than the other.

"Yeah...and your expectations were spot-on. After being skewered like a sardine last time, I swore to skewer you back..."

Pitohui responded to his snarl with a vicious smile of her own. "Very nice. I suppose I'll have to fillet you this time."

"Shut up!"

David was the first to move again. As he rushed her, he started to slash from the right again—only to stop one step short and abruptly spin.

"Shaaa!"

He slashed down toward Pitohui's right shoulder with the momentum of his rotation.

Bshak! She did not buy his feint—and raised her blade with both arms to block him from cutting her in two.

This time, Pitohui's physical strength won out. David's lightsword bounced back up, and she made a thrusting pose—but did not follow through.

"Whoa!"

That was because David had rotated the handle of the lightsword in the hand holding it high, so he could swing it down backhanded. If Pitohui had taken one step closer, it would have skewered her right through the head.

Exactly like the sardine he announced he would make her.

After two exchanges, the duel was not yet over. David and Pitohui distanced themselves again and exhaled at nearly the same moment.

"Phew…"

"Wheeew…"

David slowly lifted his sword arm and rotated the weapon in his hand to return to a forehand grip. As he did so, he glanced at the little silver tube.

"Aha! So you noticed." Pitohui grinned at him.

"Same goes for yours," David said, showing his canines. Pitohui opened her hand to display the silver tube in her palm. There was a tiny little display panel on the side.

The bar graph on the display showed the energy reserve of the lightsword. A player could see that information in the lower-right corner of their field of vision, but it was quicker to glance directly into one's hands and didn't take your eyes off the enemy as much.

The energy level of both swords was almost exactly the same: nearly depleted. The displays were red, indicating just a few percent of overall power left.

"And you don't have a backup energy pack, do you?" she taunted. "Though I'll admit, they're a pain in the ass to exchange."

"Hmph!"

"The energy expenditure of a photon sword is based on the length of time its blade has been out. And when they slash against each other, that also eats up a ton of power. Did you know that?"

"Are you saying…you knew that, and you got me to cut down the wires to the evacuation boats on purpose?"

"What if I did?"

"Well, it puts you in the same…boat!" he yelled, rushing forward even quicker on the third attempt.

"*Teiyaa!*" he screamed, rushing in with the blade overhead. He swung down with all of his fury and power, determined to finish the fight with this blow. The red sword rushed at Pitohui's head, set to cleave it in two.

"*Sei!*" Pitohui turned her sword sideways with both hands to block it.

"*Daraaa!*" David had more than one swing in him. Two, three times he smashed at the same spot in succession.

"Rgh!" With each sizzling impact, Pitohui was pushed a bit farther back, and the angle at which her lightsword blocked it decreased.

"Daaa!" On the fourth strike, Pitohui's lightsword lost the battle, and its tip pointed down to the floor of the bridge.

"I've got youuuu!" David's fifth swing headed straight for Pitohui's unprotected face.

Bshak! Again, the two swords were joined in a tussle of strength.

"Wha—?!"

"You see? You got so worked up that you forgot about the last time."

Though the lightsword hilt in Pitohui's hand was still tilted downward, the glowing blue blade was now extending from the bottom end rather than the top.

It was a feature of her Muramasa F9 that the control dial could be spun in either direction to make it emerge from either side of the tube. That was how David got speared through the brain last time.

"Shit!" he swore, gnashing his teeth.

Once again, they were locked in a struggle, David with normal downward grip and Pitohui with a backhand from below. The image was similar to their final duel in SJ2, except that there had been only one sword that time.

Their strength evened out, and they were deadlocked. The blades crackled where they intersected. In the meantime, their energy levels plummeted.

The blades of light began to shrink at last, shortening at nearly the same time and speed. They had no more than ten seconds left.

"So we'll end it with a fistfight! That suits me perfectly fine!"

"What, you like punching women? I'm not into violent guys like that."

Even as the deadlock sapped the last moments of their lightswords, they traded verbal jabs.

"Like...like you're one to talk!"

"Well, I'll pass on the fistfight idea."

"I won't give you time to surrender!"

Their blades were no more than eight inches long now, more like daggers. With so much less shining-light surface to go around, they could actually view each other's faces better.

That's when David saw Pitohui smile—a pleased, utterly wicked smile.

"The biggest downside of lightswords is that they're stupidly expensive, but the biggest upsides are that they can cut anything, and…"

Just before the blades went out, both combatants leaped away from each other.

As they did, they let go of the hilts together. Two swords clattered to the floor, nothing but tubes now.

"Daaaa!"

David gingerly clenched his fingers and swung a blow with the base of his palm.

"…They're light to use!" Pitohui finished, reaching behind her back with both hands and pulling them forward again.

In her right hand, a lightsword.

In her left hand, a photon sword.

In other words, she was dual-wielding sabers. She had two extras hiding in her little backpack.

"—!"

But there was no stopping his momentum now.

David plunged straight toward her, so Pitohui neatly stepped backward and swung her arms in front of herself, right to left and left to right. Then she swiftly whipped her arms back outward and inward once more, for a total of three attacks.

Head, face, neck, chest, stomach, waist, thighs.

His avatar body split into many pieces at once. And with a last scream of wrathful loathing, David exited the SJ3 battlefield.

"You sick, bourgeois bastaaaard!!"

David tumbled to the ground in horizontal pieces like the end of a block-balancing game, red damage lines along the cuts.

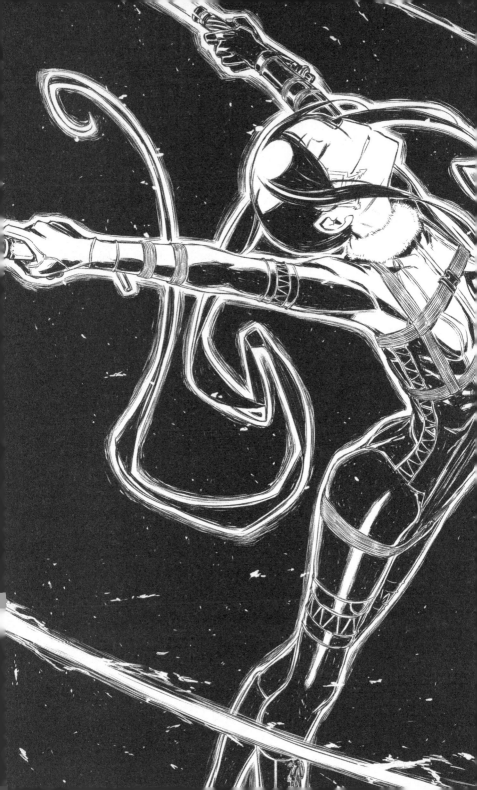

"Ah! Crap!" Pitohui shouted, looking panicked with the light-swords in her hands. "I forgot; I said I was gonna fillet him! I was supposed to slice him *vertically!* I'm so stupid!"

It was a feature of Squad Jam that bodies didn't remain in place in a gory aftermath, so the pieces of David's body shone as they silently gathered together into the peaceful form of the recently departed, faceup on the ground. The DEAD tag floated over his body.

Alone on the bridge, Pitohui waved her left hand in the air to call up her menu, then chose to materialize her entire preset of gear in her inventory, returning her to her full outfit.

The headgear appeared on top, her bulletproof vest was next, then the XDM pistols on either thigh, the M870 Breacher at her left side, and lastly, the KTR-09 appeared in her hands.

Once she had them on her person, Pitohui wobbled and fell onto her bottom. "Whoops…"

She exhaled and murmured, "Phew, this is rough… I feel kinda sick, actually. I think I'm gonna throw up."

"I believe you require rest," Clara said with concern. *"Please don't neglect your physical condition."*

"Oh, I'm fine…"

Pitohui got up using the KTR-09 as a crutch, then swung it on the shoulder sling. She got her feet going, scooped up David's STM-556, and moved over to the console area.

"You have no presently designated destination," said the system. *"Where shall we go now?"*

Pitohui replied, "Well, Clara, why don't you take me across the River Styx to the Third Street of Hell?"

"I have no port registered under that name."

"It's right here," Pitohui said, propping the STM-556 against her shoulder and firing five shots into the console in a semiauto burst.

"Please stop. I will lose functionality," Clara said in the same tone she'd been using previously.

"I know."

Pitohui continued shooting. The active monitors went dark as bullets pierced and shattered them.

"Please stop. I will lose functionality. Please stop. I will lose functionality. Please stop. I will lose functionality."

"Oh, just go to sleep already," she said, emptying the thirty-round magazine.

"Yes, ma'am. Good night," said Clara, and she fell silent for eternity.

It was 1:39.

"No-hyo?"

Llenn gasped when the ship suddenly lurched as she skulked in the Deck 6 hallway, waiting for the 1:40 scan to arrive. Aside from having to continually go up floors to escape the rising water, it had been a smooth voyage until the ground shook under her feet just now.

It was an unpleasant kind of shaking, too, tilting and rocking, like standing atop a board placed on a balancing ball.

"What now?" Fukaziroh murmured. She was sitting on the carpet, arms around her knees, spacing out because nothing else was happening. "It's like we're on a boat!"

We are *on a boat*, Llenn thought.

"This isn't good," M commented. "Feels like we're losing stability."

"What do you mean…? Are we gonna sink?" Llenn asked.

"That's possible."

No sooner were the words out of M's mouth than the interior of the ship lurched and tilted. This time it was a forward motion, the nose tipping down with a sensation like car brakes being slammed.

"Hyooo!"

The water had been below the stairs moments ago, but now it splashed into the hallway. Llenn's group was already drenched from the sprinkler water, so getting wetter wasn't a problem now, as long as it didn't involve drowning. The water level rose and rose.

"Run! Go up!" M commanded.

"But the scan—," Llenn protested. Her boots were already submerged, and the damage effect was starting to kick in. If she stayed there, she was either going to drown or suffer damage until she died.

As the trio started up the stairs, the deck they'd been on mere seconds ago was being swallowed by the cloudy murk. The air being displaced by all that water flooding into the interior blew past their damp skin, causing a chill.

"How high are we going to go, M?!"

"As far up as we can!"

"But won't Pito be watching the scan and waiting for us?"

"Probably."

"Then—"

"You wanted to talk to her, didn't you?" said M.

"Yeah, so it's perfect!" Fukaziroh chimed in.

"I know, but—! Arrgh! Shit!" Llenn swore, tensing. Then she burst forward, fast enough to leave the other two behind—and indeed did—as she rushed up the rocking stairs.

The time was 1:40.

On the terminal device's screen, Pitohui saw Llenn and company moving up the stairs as she maintained balance on the rocking floor of the bridge.

Then she said to herself, "I'll need to welcome them. Where should I do that?"

Since there were no battle scenes happening, the stream in the pub gave them a rare long-distance shot of the cruise ship racing across gray seas.

"Whoa! Is it tilting forward?"

The audience noticed something was wrong.

"That's true... Did it start taking on more water when it hit the building?"

"Nah, it's been in the process of sinking ever since the start."

As that person said, the waterline had been rising up the side of the ship for a while, but it was harder to notice the problem when Clara was actively managing the balance of the craft.

The balance of the ship between fore and aft was called trim. With the front of the ship tilting downward, that meant it had "positive trim." The cruise ship, dented prow and all, continued to kick up waves at top speed, but it was clear to the naked eye that it was leaning quite a bit. The state of the ship was obviously abnormal.

"I don't want it to sink before the final battle and have there be cochampions because everyone drowned at the same time..."

"Yeah! We're here to watch a death match!"

"The two remaining teams are Pitohui and Eva; and Llenn, Fukaziroh, and M."

"Two versus three..."

On another screen, Llenn's group was climbing up the stairs. Just then, she finished clearing ten-plus floors and emerged on Deck 17. This was the deck with the wide-open space and the bridge at one end.

From the inside, Llenn had a better sense of the ship's current state than anyone.

It was tilting forward at the moment—and wobbling irregularly. The scary thing was that it was still rushing forward at full speed.

Between the holes in the sides, the huge hole Fukaziroh accidentally put in it, and the damage to the prow from smashing into the building, it was anyone's guess how much water was entering the ship every second.

But for now, all she could do was keep moving.

She'd left Fukaziroh and M behind and gone as far up the stairs as they would take her: Deck 17.

When Llenn burst out into the wide-open space, she was greeted by a smiling Pitohui.

"Hi there! Long time no see!"

"Eek!" Llenn shrieked, readying her P90 on reflex. "......"

But she did not shoot.

They were in a spacious hall. It was an open, flat space, dozens of yards to a side. Here and there were load-bearing pillars to hold up more construction.

Whatever had been here once, the refugees had probably taken it out. The area was totally empty. Here and there on the red carpet were dark stains a foot or two across. Either someone had spilled something...or someone's blood had been spilled there.

The room was quite dark. There wasn't a single window here, on the inside of the ship. Only a third of the lights on the ceiling were on; the rest had been removed, probably for use elsewhere.

Pitohui stood leaning back against one of the pillars. The KTR-09 was slung at her side, and there was nothing in her hands. She was about a hundred feet away.

Llenn with her P90 in position, Pitohui with her hands dangling. They faced each other in silence for about five seconds.

"Oh? You aren't going to shoot me? You're so nice, Llenn," Pitohui drawled, totally unconcerned.

"Pito!" Llenn shouted, loud enough to echo across the entire hall. She was furious.

"Whoa! There she is. Oh, hey! Been a while!" came another careless voice, after the sound of footsteps tromping up the stairs behind her.

"Hey again, Fuka!" said Pitohui, waving.

Last came M, and though he didn't say anything, Pito gave him a bracing "Yo! You survived. That's some good fighting; well done."

Then she peeled off of the pillar and took a few steps against the tilt of the ship that was getting even more pronounced and spread her arms.

"Well, here we are. LPFM versus Betrayers, but now it's three on one. What do you say, Llenn? Shall we?"

There was something Llenn really wanted to ask Pitohui.
It was why she had struggled to survive this far.
Yet, she no longer needed to ask it.

"Three on one... I knew it! I knew it! I...I knew it!" Llenn screamed to the ceiling.

"You knew it?"

"You knew what?" Fukaziroh and M asked their teammate.

"Oh, I get it! So this is what you were thinking the whole time, Llenn," Pitohui said, smirking as she walked closer. "What if the betrayers' team actually got *two* members from our squad?"

"......"

Llenn said nothing. Pitohui crossed the red carpet, her boots pressing into the surface.

"Uh-huh, uh-huh, uh-huh," she murmured. "Well, Llenn, I'll admit, the possibility is higher than zero."

"......"

Pitohui walked past Llenn and approached Fukaziroh and M instead. "But this possibility is much more likely: that I was just a huge liar."

"......"

Fukaziroh then let go of her grenade launchers and let them hang from her shoulders. Then she smacked her fist into her palm. Apparently, she'd let go specifically to perform this gesture.

"I see! And that's why it's three on one! Meaning that Pito and M and I are on LPFM, and Llenn is on Team Betrayer!"

"So are you saying you weren't actually chosen, Pito?" asked M.

"Did you see the evidence?"

"Hmm?"

"Did anyone actually see the message on my device that clearly stated *You are a betrayer*?"

M had no choice but to shake his head. Fukaziroh added, "You know, you're right. I didn't see it."

Pitohui was standing next to Fukaziroh and M now. Llenn turned around and faced the three at a distance of a few dozen feet.

"At first, it was mostly a joke. I mean, it had to be, right? I had no idea that the weird flying thingy was going to let a person who wasn't picked ride it anyway. If I wasn't allowed to get on, I'd stick out my tongue and go 'Whoopsie, turns out I wasn't picked after all!'"

"But you were able to ride it."

"That's right, Fuka. It gave me the room to just barge my way right into the betrayers' team. Was it a loophole in the game system? Or was that another intentional feature of *GGO*, the game where participants can even kill their own squadmates? I met up with the other betrayers, and we started our own party. I was able to fight alongside them."

"Other members of BTRY died on the ship. Did you do that, Pito?" M asked, still calm and collected.

"I did, M. In fact, I sliced one of them into ribbons earlier!" said Pitohui happily.

"Wow, Pito! That sounds like a major accomplishment!" bubbled Fukaziroh.

It all made Llenn wonder *What in the world was I doing, then...?*

The entire battle flashed back through her mind.

First of all, she hadn't wanted to enter SJ3 at all. Her only reason for registering was to fulfill her promise to Boss. That hadn't worked out at all.

She appeared on the same team with Pitohui so she wouldn't have to fight her, and she ended up as an enemy anyway. The nasty sponsor's betrayers' team rule just added a lot of headache to her experience in the end.

Whose fault is all of this?

Is it my fault?

No, not at all.

The old Llenn probably would have jumped to the simplistic conclusion that, yes, it was her own fault. Then she would have gone into a sulky mood, claiming *Oh, boo-hoo, I was born only to suffer like this...*

But after all the battles she'd been through, Llenn had toughened up, in ways good and bad, and now she no longer thought that way.

She wanted to beat the stupid writer half to death, but really, the biggest cause of trouble this time around started with the letter *P* and ended in *I*.

"Gosh, have I just been the star of this whole event? Tell me more! Sing my praises!"

The one with the tattoos on her cheeks, smiling blissfully and chattering to herself.

This asshole.

"Y-you...asshole..."

She finally spoke her thoughts aloud.

"Exsqueeze me? Did you say something, Llenn?"

"Yes, I did."

"What was it?"

"Pito, you're an asshole! Why would you do such a thing?!"

"Well, uh..." Pitohui shrugged her shoulders theatrically, grinned, and said, "Wouldn't you say this is *your* fault for being fooled that easily?"

Snap!

Llenn felt something inside her mind give way. It was the last of her patience.

Her little body began to tremble. Because her agility level was so high, even her shivering seemed to happen faster. It was so rapid that it created an afterimage, a blurring of her outline.

After trembling for roughly 2.58 seconds, Llenn sucked in a

deep breath and yelled, "Pitooooo! I'm gonna kill you! This is the perfect chance! You're my enemy, so I don't need to show you mercy! Or forgiveness! Just defeat!"

"Ooh, scary! So scary! Gimme all ya got! That's what I want—it's why I tricked you like this! It's true!"

"I really will beat you! I'll seriously beat you! I'll beat you right now! I'm gonna make you cry!"

"Come on and do it, if you can! You're welcome anytime!"

The two women bellowed at each other, pure competition pulsing out of them. It was a screaming match between two people armed with guns.

Suddenly, Pitohui lowered her voice and said with mock concern, "Oh, but three on one is kind of unfair, don't you think? What should we do?"

"Urgh…" Llenn clenched her jaw so hard, her teeth felt likely to break.

"No, it's three on two," said someone else.

A bright-yellow light shone in the dark space, passing between Llenn and the other three. They momentarily lost their ability to see.

"Turn around and run!" said a voice. Llenn did as it commanded. She couldn't see, but she did not hesitate. It was an all-out sprint.

"Wha—?! Oh, shoot!" Pitohui hissed. She took the KTR-09 down from her shoulder right as the second signal flare passed before her eyes.

The flares were meant to be clearly visible against the distant, cloudy sky. So what happened if it passed ten feet in front of your face? Nothing but afterimage burned into your eyes.

"Dammit!" Pitohui yelped, and she gave up on aiming her KTR-09.

"Aaah… My eyes! Myize!" Fukaziroh said, running about in a panic. "Is Llenn running away? Can I shoot? Can I shoot now?"

"No way! Are you trying to kill *all* of us?!" snapped M, who remained logical even when he couldn't see. He had no choice but to stop her. Fukaziroh was more than capable of firing another plasma grenade in this situation.

"Dammit! I was so fixated on Llenn that I forgot about Evaaaaaa!" wailed Pitohui, who seemed to be sincere in this regard. She hunched down in a defensive position. "I'm just not in my right mind today... I'm so stupid, stupid, stupid!"

A third, then fourth flare shot through the space over her head.

CHAPTER 16

SECT.16

Save the Last Battle for Me

CHAPTER 16
Save the Last Battle for Me

Llenn raced through the vast hall at top speed without any vision. Her sheer physical ability carried her at speeds no other person could match, blazing across the open floor until she slammed into one of the pillars.

"Hrbegya!"

Fortunately, it wasn't a head-on collision, so she bounced off to the left.

"Gaaah!"

Her momentum pulled her into a roll.

"Gubh!"

The rotation carried her all the way to the edge of the space, where she hit the wall and came to a stop.

"Come! Grab hold!" said a familiar voice from very close by.

"Okay…," Llenn mumbled, dizzy and in pain all over. She obeyed the voice and saw through slowly recovering eyes the blurry image of a large hand reaching out to her.

"Can you see?"

"Barely. And you, Pito?"

"I'm fine. All right, let's go and kill those two. Just the two of us in LPFM!"

"Gotcha!"

As the hall tilted further, the two women chatted happily—while they were somewhat deranged—as their eyesight improved.

"What about me?" asked the man nearby.

Pitohui's answer was instant.

"If you get in my way, I'll kill you!"

"I can see fine now. I'll be all right. Thanks, Boss…"

"There we go."

Llenn and Eva (aka Boss) were hurrying down the corridor of Deck 17 toward the stern. Boss had been pulling Llenn along by the hand, but she let go now.

It was a long hallway, running along the cabins on the port side of the ship. Though it was hard to tell because there were no windows, the incline was a gentle upward climb.

"We want as much distance as possible. Then we'll wait for the scan. It's about one…forty-four right now. We might not get the chance to see the next scan in time," said Boss. She wasn't slow, but obviously she couldn't keep up with Llenn.

So the smaller girl followed behind her and muttered, "I'm sorry for…all kinds of stuff."

In her hand was the Satellite Scanner. She scrolled the screen until it showed a clear, unmistakable message: *You are a betrayer.*

When the messages had gone out, she got so distracted by Pitohui's joke that she never checked for herself, and she allowed Pitohui to take over the role she herself was meant to play. Because of that, she wasn't able to have the direct confrontation with SHINC she wanted.

All of this demanded an apology.

"I'm…so sorry…," she repeated.

Boss didn't turn around. "Look, it's fine."

"But—!"

This time, Boss looked over her shoulder as she ran, and on her craggy face was the sweetest smile.

"We're on the same team now, aren't we?"

*   *   *

1:45.

Pitohui and Fukaziroh watched Llenn and Eva's movement on the terminal screen.

"They're running away! C'mon, come and fight us!" Fukaziroh said, incensed.

"But of course they are," said Pitohui, calm and rational.

They ran and ran and ran, but the 1,600-foot ship would never end. Doors passed on the right and left as they ran up the hill that was the hallway.

The bigger and slower of the two said, "The slope is getting tougher, slowly but surely. The prow is dipping, so the stern goes up. Eventually, it won't be able to stay intact, and the entire ship will crack in half, with the front end pulling downward and sinking."

It was a remarkably accurate summary of the physical forces at work. For a teenage girl, she had quite a lot of knowledge about ships.

"I was on a site for classic movies recently and watched DiCaprio's *Titanic*, so I know how it works," she explained. "So what now, Llenn? If we keep running toward the stern and find a hiding place, or if we protect the stern and keep them at bay, we could force them to drown instead."

The smaller one answered, "Yeah. If we kill them, we win."

"I thought you'd say that."

They ran past a wall upon which was scrawled the message *We'll live, survive, and create a world without war this time!*

"…So she said."

M had never turned off his comm unit, so he pulled it loose to relate Llenn's words to the other two.

"Uh-oh, did we wake the sleeping child?" Pitohui wondered aloud, sitting on the floor of the empty hall.

"A bit late for that, Pito." Fukaziroh smirked. "Was that a joke? Besides, we can just put her to bed *permanently* on this ship instead."

They had finished prepping themselves for action. Pitohui had every magazine she could possibly hold now present on her person. The KTR-09 had a drum magazine with a full seventy-five rounds. The two lightswords were placed within easy access of her hands. Only the M870 Breacher shotgun was left on the ground with holster and all.

Fukaziroh's double MGL-140s were fully loaded with grenades from her backpack. The first two in Leftania were the plasma grenades that could destroy the ship itself.

Also, she was no longer hauling that heavy backpack around. There were a few backup grenades in pouches on her bulletproof combat vest. Her M&P pistol was on her thigh, not that she could accurately shoot anyone with it.

"I wasn't hearing Llenn's voice anymore. They must have noticed and rearranged the team over there," M reported. "Are you sure you don't want me to take part in this?"

"Stop asking, M. Who wants to win a fight with a three-on-two advantage? Would you rather die right here?" Pitohui replied, pretending to point the KTR-09 at M. It had to be pretend, because otherwise she would have shot him. Pitohui didn't point her guns at people she didn't mean to shoot.

"If you mess with Llenn, I'll kill you. Got that? It's an order," she told him. "All you have left is the job of crowning the 'true winner' at the end. Now give me that."

In a private cabin, Team Betrayers was properly reregistered, making sure that Llenn's communication device was connected to Boss instead.

"I'm going with this and the knife only. No grenades. You?" she asked, gesturing with the P90.

Boss replied, "Vintorez and Strizh. And a combat knife, in

imitation of you. I didn't have much time to practice with it, though. A few grenades, too."

"Ooh," Llenn murmured, her eyes sparkling dangerously. "Any plasmas in there?"

"Yes. I've got twelve, since I was carrying for my whole team. I just had them in my item storage before, because I was afraid of them getting set off."

"Any grand grenades?"

"Same. Half dozen."

Grand grenade was a player-derived nickname. It was a massive plasma grenade with devastating power on par with Fukaziroh's launcher grenades. It could obliterate everything within sixty feet of its blast.

But as Boss said, "They're pretty much unusable inside the ship."

The grand grenade was the poster child of *GGO* weapons that were ultrapowerful—but with major drawbacks. Fukaziroh's launchers were safer in comparison, because they would only shoot if it was going to travel a safe distance. Now that she was an enemy, those last two plasma grenades were a frightening thing to consider. Between the signals and pushing back the sea, it was probably a very good thing for Llenn that Fuka had already used three of them.

Llenn thought it over, muttering to herself. "With this firepower... If we want to make sure we beat the two of them... Don't have much time... How do we win, how do we win, how do we...?"

Boss decided not to cut her off. She waited.

"How do we win...? How do we...?"

Llenn's eyes stopped doing circles and froze still. She turned to Boss.

"Give me a grand grena— No, all your plasma grenades."

The huge crowd in the bar, including those competitors who had already died and returned to the main room, were about to witness the final battle of SJ3.

On the monitors, the ship was rudderless, still blazing along madly. Over half the prow was under the water now, producing tremendous waves along the sides. The five-hundred-yard ship was leaning far forward, and the stern was quite high up. The froth whipped up by the relentless screw propellers was even busier than usual. But based on the state of the tilt, it wasn't likely to sink in the next five or ten minutes.

The camera angle switched.

"Oh-ho!"

"Here we go!"

Two female players were walking through the vast courtyard of Deck 10. Around them were abandoned storefronts and rusted amusement park rides. But they walked boldly right through the spacious center area, guns in hand.

Pitohui had her KTR-09. Fukaziroh had her MGL-140s, Rightony in her right hand and Leftania hanging from her left shoulder.

Both held a shield in their off hands, positioned out in front of their bodies. They were part of M's shield.

The unfolding shield was made of eight plates measuring twenty inches tall and twelve inches wide. They had reconfigured them into personal shields of four plates each. There must be handles on the back for them to hold.

With a shield three feet tall and over a foot and a half wide, even Pitohui could defend a considerable part of her front—to say nothing of tiny Fukaziroh. Now they could walk out in the open around their foe and not have to worry about an insta-kill shot.

"That should protect them against Llenn's P90, obviously, and even Eva's Vintorez sniper rifle."

"Oh, I can feel it! Shield soldiers! It's gonna be the new thing!"

"They can only do this because they both have tons of strength! That's not something most players can pull off!"

On the screen, Pitohui and Fukaziroh climbed the hilly road, chatting enjoyably. The battle would be at the top of the hill.

"It's almost like a date. Oh, they laughed!"

"What are they talking about?"

"I'm sure it's the strategy for how they plan to obliterate Llenn and Eva."

No matter how pristine the video footage was, there were certain things that couldn't be displayed on the screen.

Such as a trembling fist holding the shield handle. Only Fukaziroh, with her close proximity, could detect something like that.

She brought up the sole conclusion that could be reached.

"Pito?"

"What is it, Fuka?"

"I can tell, you know."

"Tell what?"

"That you're scared of Llenn."

Fukaziroh was parallel with her, facing forward to keep an eye out, so she did not catch Pitohui's smirking grin.

They traded words as they walked, but not glances.

"In all my time playing VR games, there are only two times I've thought *This person is stronger than me. Not just in terms of skill, but mentally, too.*"

"Only? That's happened at least twenty times for me. Sorry, I mean two hundred. So when was the first time, Pito?"

"Right after I started playing games. When I was a beta tester for *Sword Art Online*. It was the first real VR game in the world, so everyone was starting from the same conditions. But there were plenty of people there who were better than me. I ended up dueling one of them over the right to fight a monster that dropped a specific piece of loot. It was some beta-male pretty boy who thought he was so cool."

"And you lost and got killed?"

"No. When my hit points were almost gone, the guy said, 'It's impressive that you can do that well, two levels below me. You can take the boss here. Let's fight again once we're the same level, heh, *swish-sparkle.*' And then he put away his sword."

"My goodness."

"And if you'll allow me to brag, he took a lot of damage, too. But in the midst of this fight to the death, he goes and acts all cool and cocky. At the time, all I thought about was powering myself up. I was ashamed of how weak I was. I reflected on my faults and realized I wasn't good enough."

"Yep. Reflection makes you stronger."

"So I thought, when the game launches in full, I'll fight that guy again and totally PK his ass…"

"But you just missed out on playing the full game, didn't you, Pito? That probably saved his life."

"Or…maybe mine."

They walked past the spot where MMTM had been electrocuted. The tiled path, which was designed to look like cobblestones, was still wet. They had another 250 yards to reach the stern. The angle of their ascent was gently rising.

It was 1:48. No sign of movement from the enemy team.

"The other person, of course, was Llenn. The first time I saw her, I was mostly stunned at the way her core was rock-solid. She's got an astonishing sense of balance."

"I see. Well, since we're here, I might as well tell you that before Kohi grew like a weed, she was really athletic. I heard it from her older sister. Whenever the two of them did some kind of exercise together, she always wanted to copy her big sister, and she learned how to do things right away."

"I can tell. If she didn't have a thing about her height and really worked hard to learn a sport under an excellent coach, she could have been an Olympic athlete for Japan right now."

"When I heard Kohi say she was going to play VR games, I was really looking forward to what kind of character she would grow into…but it seems like she 'grew too much' over here, too."

"Ha-ha-ha. Well, I always wanted to have a real, honest duel with Llenn, so when it came true last time, I was extremely happy about it."

"And you lost."

"Thanks to *someone's* very precise help."

"Ohhh? Who could that be?"

"When she bit down on my throat, I thought I was going to die. I thought I'd actually die. That it was all over for good. I thought it was a worthy end for me. And in the end…I didn't die."

"Like you sucked it up and jumped in front of a train, only to fall flat and have it pass over your head?"

"Kinda. Some other stuff happened around then, too, but in short, I decided that if I wound up alive anyway, I might as well take good care of that life…"

The trembling in Pitohui's left hand stopped.

"But I'm still scared when I see that little pink shrimp."

In the middle of the courtyard was an information board with a monitor set up next to a large flower planter. It had that huge *i* mark on it for identification.

As 1:49 approached, they stopped there. The two squatted next to the barren planter, hid behind their shields, and Fukaziroh pulled out her device while Pitohui acted as spotter.

"I see. So, to you, she's kind of like a source of trauma that you have to beat and get past."

"Oh, it's not nearly as noble as that. It's just a grudge. Hatred. She's someone I want to beat the crap out of, that's all."

"Ooooh. Well, I'm here for you, Miss Pito, Miss Elza."

"Thanks. You sure, though? She's your good friend, right? I'd be pretty sad if you ended up fighting over this in real life."

"If we were going to break up over something like this, we would have run the rivers of northern Japan red with blood already. The truth is we're bound by such tight friendship, I don't even want to point a gun at Llenn. How often do you think we fought at the all-girls high school we went to?"

"I couldn't guess, but it sounds like a good story. You'll have to tell me later."

"You could probably write a song about it."

"Well, what a delight."

"And you'll invite me to your concert, as the provider of the original song inspiration, of course. With airfare paid and all."

"As long as you bring Llenn with you, you're welcome anytime."

"But she's so uptight, I don't know…"

"What, are you assuming that I'm going to try to sleep with her?"

1:49 and forty seconds.

Two people traded words through their remote earpieces.

"Let's go, Boss!"

"Okay, Llenn!"

1:49 and forty-nine seconds.

"So where are they gonna be now?" Fukaziroh wondered, waving the Satellite Scan terminal next to the *i* on the wall. Pitohui kept an eye out for their surroundings, particularly in the aft direction of the ship.

The scan started from the top of the ship, going down one floor per second.

"What?" It showed the location of the enemy. Fukaziroh reported, "Eva's on Deck Ten. Port side, near the stern, two hundred yards ahead of us. Llenn's on the same deck, two hundred yards behind us. Right at the tip of the courtyard!"

Pitohui murmured, "They split up…?"

It was an impossible strategy, in a variety of senses.

For one thing, why would they isolate their valuable firepower individually? It would be a two-on-one fight if Pitohui and Fukaziroh went after one of them—a massive disadvantage to them.

For another, it made no sense that Llenn would head toward the prow, behind their current location. She'd probably gone down the hallway past the cabins to circle around. But if she ran away from them once, why rush back?

What was more, she would have had plenty of chances to attack them in the courtyard as she passed the cabins. Why hadn't she?

On the other hand, Llenn's sharpshooting ability was limited. But while she might not have been able to kill both at once, she probably could have managed to take out Pitohui, at least.

So if Llenn hadn't gone mad with terror, there was only one possibility.

"Be careful, Fuka. They're planning something big."

"Okay, will do. You seem to be enjoying yourself, Pito."

"Oh, you can tell?"

M watched and waited, listening to Pitohui and Fukaziroh chat through his earpiece.

He was on the roof of the passenger cabins on the starboard side, close to the center of the ship. The backpack was no longer over his shoulders.

Within his view of the courtyard below, right at the entrance to the open space, was a small, fast-moving pink blur. The distance between them was less than seven hundred feet, even accounting for elevation. It was an easy distance to hit a target with his M14 EBR. He could have shot her at any moment.

"……"

But he said nothing and did nothing, except watch what Llenn did.

This is bad, he thought, and he took off running for the stern of the ship with all the speed he could muster.

There was a blast behind them, and the sound and vibration rocked their brains and bodies.

"Nwuh?" "Whoa?"

The first thing Pitohui and Fukaziroh did was lower themselves further to the ground. Anyone accustomed to battle knew that wherever the blast was, the first thing you did was get down to make yourself a smaller target for any potential shrapnel.

That was when they saw, farther down the gentle slope of the courtyard, a writhing ball of blue flame where Llenn had been a moment before. It looked like some enormous living thing trying to swallow the ship from below. The pale-blue beast expanded, and when it started to vanish, it bulged again, changing into odd forms.

"Could that be...?!" Fukaziroh yelped. She recognized that surging blue light.

"Yes, it could... They did it, dammit!"

The sound of metal breaking and air rumbling echoed off the surface of the cabin structures on either side, creating a deafening roar in the courtyard.

The rumbling lasted for over fifteen seconds, sending quakes through the earth—make that the ship.

*   *   *

Even before that, the audience had seen what Llenn was doing.

What kind of nonsense she was pulling, more precisely.

A few minutes earlier, while hiding in the passenger room closest to the stern, Llenn gave her own weapon to Eva. The one gun she owned, the P90. She also removed all the magazines she had, from her waist pouches and inventory.

In exchange, Boss gave her six objects about the size of small watermelons: grand grenades. And in addition to that, twelve of the normal, cylindrical plasma grenades thrown by hand.

With them all safe in her virtual storage, Llenn rushed off without a moment's hesitation. She blazed down the port-side cabin hallway at nearly twenty-five miles per hour. From the camera following her from behind, it looked like a warp scene from a sci-fi movie.

She didn't stop moving until she got to where the courtyard ended.

The fore end of the ship was significantly submerged now. Deck 10 hadn't been baptized yet, but based on the angle of the ship, the seawater had to be up to about Deck 7 or 8 by now.

It was at this point that she engaged in something that would cause any ship owner to faint.

She pulled the grand grenades back out of her inventory and

activated them. By carefully setting the timers, she arranged them to go off at thirty seconds past 1:50, at intervals of three seconds.

Then she rolled them out into the courtyard. They were spaced out in neat arrangement, so that they would cross the entire width of the courtyard. She also put the ordinary plasma grenades among them—these would go off when caught in the blasts.

The preparation was careful. All that was left was for her to escape.

Llenn sprinted like a rabbit back up the corridor.

"So, uh, what does this mean?" one observer wondered.

"They're going to blow in a second," someone else answered.

"Yeah, no crap! What I mean is: What's gonna happen to the ship when all those things go off?!"

"We're about to find out."

The blue explosion roared and thrashed like a giant creature.

It ripped aside the hardy steel decks of the ship like tissue paper, throwing scraps high into the air.

With each blast, the entire ship shook, such that the vibration even formed extra waves coming off its sides.

Once the series of explosions was completely done, there was nothing but a giant hole left behind. The surface of the courtyard was simply gouged away, exposing the interior structure of the ship to easy observation.

Huge waves of seawater poured through the hole, from the sides and the bottom. It was like a waterfall going through. The forward-tilting ship now creaked and warped at that spot.

The sound of the metal screeching was like a bellowing scream. A huge new fissure appeared vertically up the sides of the ship, and when it had traveled all the way around... *Crack.*

The 1,600-foot-long ship broke into two pieces.

The front portion, about five hundred of those feet, and the rear, the other 1,100—never to meet again.

The front of the ship sank at a higher speed than before. Waves lashed at the helipad, and it soon went under. Next, the bridge plunged into the water, taking with it the inactive Clara, down to a place where she would never see the sun again.

The rear part of the ship, however, temporarily regained level balance after it snapped. But the massive influx of water where it broke and the surface waves washing over the flat courtyard area did not allow them much time to relax.

Now it was the 1,100-foot rear length of the ship that began to list forward, more and more.

"Stupid Llenn! Are you trying to drown us?! Was that awesome show of spirit earlier just a lie?!" fumed Fukaziroh, who clearly understood the intent of the stunt.

"Hya-ha-ha-ha-ha! That's the Llenn I know!" Pitohui cackled for some reason.

A huge amount of seawater was rushing toward them from the bottom of the hilly slope.

"Oh well. Guess we gotta move forward."

"Dammit!"

They stood up and began to trot, holding their shields in front of them. Naturally, they were heading for the stern.

Gwang!

There was the sound of metal being heavily, violently pierced.

"Ugh!" Fukaziroh came to a stop.

Sparks burst from the shield in her hands in rapid succession. She dropped to a crouch, angling the shield and pulling her left arm to cover her side so she could withstand the shots to the best of her ability.

With each pang against the shield, sparks appeared, and Fukaziroh's body slid backward. There was no gunshot sound at all.

"It's Eva!"

Pitohui leaned to the right, holding up the shield on her left, and opened fire with the KTR-09.

She could barely aim it shooting with one hand; this was mostly to put pressure on the area where she saw the bullet lines coming from.

Boss's silent sniping came to an end. Perhaps she had withdrawn. According to the lines, she'd been shooting from the fan-shaped outdoor theater at the very end of the ship, about six hundred feet away.

"Let's crush her ass!"

It was time to fight back. Fukaziroh placed the end of the MGL-140 on the lip of the shield she held with her other hand.

Three cute consecutive shots—*pomp-pomp-pomp!*—delivered three 40 mm grenades. They shot at the speed of a BB gun pellet, 250 feet a second, in a parabolic trajectory.

Explosions and black smoke issued from where they landed, nearly all at once.

"How was that? Did I get her?" Fukaziroh asked.

Pitohui grimaced and said, "Probably not. All Eva wants to do is slow us down."

"So she can meet up with Llenn again, huh? Dammit. Should we go into a cabin?"

"If we surround ourselves with walls, we'll be helpless once the water gets to us. And we can't make use of your offensive firepower. Don't worry, we'll keep moving forward. I'm sure Llenn will show up again."

At that moment, Llenn asked, "You okay, Boss?"

"I just got a bit of shrapnel to the leg. I can still move. Though I wasn't able to get any clean hits on them."

"Oh, good!"

She was passing by Pitohui and Fukaziroh's location, in fact—racing down the port-side hallway that she'd come down, back to the stern this time.

If she rushed out into the courtyard for a surprise attack, she might have beaten Pitohui at least, but she had no P90 now. It was a sacrifice she had to make because her encumbrance level was too low for her to sprint at top speed with all those grenades on her person otherwise.

Now she blazed back down the hallway, which was tilting more than before, so that she could fit her beloved P-chan into her palm again.

Along the way, the ship rocked left and right harder than it had before.

"Ha!"

Llenn worked with the rocking, taking a few steps along each side wall as the corridor shook around her. She maintained her momentum.

M briefly paused in his travel across Deck 19 to turn around and look to the prow of the ship—where he was met with a stunning sight.

There was a broken hunk of ship, surrounded by gray sea all around it.

At the end of the slope downward from his position was five hundred feet of prow, sinking with only the jagged ends still above the water, nose down.

From this angle, it was easy to see the interior of the ship in cross section, a view that was otherwise completely impossible. There was the hall where they met up with Pitohui, for example.

And the other 1,100 feet of ship where M stood now was noticeably tilting further and further, leaning forward toward the broken end, like a submarine going into a dive.

Even at this moment, the ship's propellers seemed to be running full bore, pushing it onward across the water. Naturally, the process was allowing quite a lot of seawater into the interior.

It was impossible to tell if the broken ship would be sinking in the next five minutes, ten minutes, or perhaps even faster. Meanwhile, down in the courtyard below, Pitohui and Fukaziroh continued their forward progress, shields up.

Their methodical march reminded him of some heavy infantry of yore.

"We did it, Llenn!"

"We did it, Boss!"

When she reached the stern, Llenn met up with Boss at a spot on the lowest part of the outdoor theater, completely invisible from the courtyard.

"Here, this is yours. And you don't have to give the other thing back. Keep it."

"Thanks!" Llenn accepted the P90 back and returned the magazines to her inventory and carrying pouches. She took three seconds to stare at her pink gun.

"What's the matter? Don't worry—I didn't take a bite."

"Oh, uh… Just noticing that P-chan isn't talking this time," Llenn noted sadly. Before, when the end of a Squad Jam approached, and she got really fired up, P-chan would speak to her, but it hadn't said a word so far.

Obviously, the gun couldn't *actually* talk—she knew it was merely an odd feeling that she was experiencing. Or at least, she hoped that was the case.

"Oh. You mean when you talk to it while in a kind of trance?"

"My gun is not an 'it'! My gun is P-chan!"

"Ha-ha-ha. Maybe that's a sign that you're keeping your cool better this time? Or maybe…"

"Maybe?"

Their enjoyable conversation was interrupted by the presence of a fat bullet line that landed right between them.

"Maybe the third P-chan just happens to be the silent type."

"Yeah. I like that idea."

They split off to the left and right, shortly before the payload of that line arrived.

"Dammit. Didn't feel that one hit!" lamented Fukaziroh.

They'd been moving forward, grappling with the fear of being sniped, with five hundred feet to go. That was a fairly short distance for a firefight in *GGO*, but there was nothing in the courtyard space ahead—no obstacles, no cover.

And the stern, where Llenn and Eva were, had an outdoor theater area that descended in rows. So not only did they have the upper ground of the slope, they also had cover to hide behind, giving them an overwhelming tactical advantage.

It was still easier for Fukaziroh to deal with because her gun lobbed grenades. Pitohui could barely even get a bullet up there because her guns shot straight.

The floor creaked and tilted further.

"Whoa."

Fukaziroh extended one foot farther for better balance, right as a bunch of bullet lines appeared around the area.

No point saving it for later!

Llenn blasted and blasted away. She had her finger holding down the trigger.

She was crouched on the tallest downward step of the theater. In other words, the boundary between the seats and the courtyard.

To keep all the empty cartridges from piling up below, she held the P90 sideways and stayed down to prevent exposing herself. P-chan growled happily, expelling the long, narrow bullets at a pace of nine hundred shots per minute.

She could clearly see Fukaziroh's and Pitohui's shields in the courtyard ahead. A number of her shots hit the shields and deflected away. They weren't going to penetrate the material, and the two people holding them were too tough to take damage.

But Llenn kept firing all the same.

The magazines she'd taken out of storage were piled up right in front of her. When she was nearly about to run out of ammo, with two or three shots left, she switched to a fresh one with nearly magician-like dexterity and continued shooting.

"Arrrgh, damn her!" Fukaziroh snapped. The air around them was full of bullet lines and bullets, pinging loudly off her shield.

The P90's fifty-bullet magazine capacity and Llenn's superhuman speed were being put to effective use. Her attacks simply would not stop.

Fukaziroh didn't have the time to stick the end of the MGL-140 around her shield. And she was too close to aim over the top. Instead, she looked to her right, at Pitohui.

Pitohui was a few yards away, also crouched behind a shield propped up by her left arm—but she was smiling.

As the bullets whizzed past them, Fukaziroh said, "You seem to be enjoying yourself."

"Yes, I am. I'm thinking of nothing but how I'm going to kill the person who's shooting at me now. In fact, it's very similar to the feeling I get onstage when my mind is occupied with singing."

"Ooh, why, that's just"—Fukaziroh had to crane her neck and lift her shield to avoid a bright-red bullet line pointing down at her head—"lovely!"

The sniper bullet glanced off her large helmet and continued onward, opening a hole in the tile floor.

"Yaaaah!"

The thick barrel of the MGL-140 grenade launcher in her right hand pointed toward a room on the port side of the ship. To a balcony near the stern, where the bullet line had come from. Where Boss was.

The two grenades she shot exploded there, shattering glass that sprinkled onto the courtyard below like snow. It did not shatter or rain any human body parts.

"Tsk. Missed again. Reloading!" Fukaziroh chirped, starting the process on Rightony.

"I knew it...," Pitohui groaned to herself.

"You knew it?" Fukaziroh repeated, propping her shield up with her shoulder and rotating the hefty open cylinder of the grenade launcher.

Llenn was firing the whole time. She hadn't actually fought much in this event, leaving her with ample ammunition. She sprayed gunfire with neither mercy nor moderation.

Pitohui's eyes raced over the surroundings as the occasional bullet pinged off her shield, and she smiled with dark glee. "It might've been difficult for Eva to shoot me at that angle—but not impossible."

She was closer to the cabins on the port side, meaning that the angle to aim at her was tighter. That meant exposing more of yourself to aim for it, inviting a counterattack.

But not impossible to pull off.

"Uh-huh. Meaning?" Fukaziroh prompted. She stuck more grenades in the large cylinder, *kapunk-kapunk-kapunk.*

"They must have agreed that it would be *Llenn* who kills me. Perhaps out of Llenn's sense of duty? Either that or a personal grudge."

"My goodness! At the end of the match and still choosing her targets! Talk about confidence! Talk about arrogance!"

"So I'm going to take advantage of that mind-set. I'll go into the cabins. I'll go after Eva—pretend to, at least."

"Ha-ha-ha! Gotcha!"

Fukaziroh stood up again, done with reloading. She had her shield up, of course, in an attempt to stick out and draw Llenn's attention and gunfire.

As hoped, the bullets concentrated on her. Several glanced off the shield, but one hit the tiles and unluckily bounced up into her leg.

"Dammit, that hurt!" she yelped, falling to her knee, but the decoy plan had been a success. Pitohui had raced off to the left into the cabins, vanishing from Fukaziroh's sight.

Llenn noticed that Pitohui was no longer in view.

"Boss, Pito took the bait. She's inside."

"Got it!"

She slammed a fresh magazine into the P90.

Then she got to her feet.

"What?! What is she doing?!" screamed someone in the bar.

"……"

Up on Deck 18, M drew a sharp breath and held it.

*   *   *

When she stood up tall and proud, Llenn exposed herself to the courtyard as a pink target.

And then she shouted, in a voice so loud it seemed impossible that it could come from such a small object:

"Fukaaaaaa! Fight meeeeeeeeee!"

CHAPTER 17
Duel

SECT.17

CHAPTER 17
Duel

"What are you trying to dooooooooooooooooooooo?!"

It was a scream encompassing all of Fukaziroh's soul.

Her reaction was only natural. Moments ago, Llenn made it look like she was going for Pitohui, and as soon as Pitohui vanished, she challenged Fukaziroh to a duel instead.

"Is this all a joke to you?!"

It was no wonder she was furious. Fukaziroh stomped through the courtyard, shield in hand. That way, she could defend against any shots—but Llenn did not shoot. She just stood, hands on her hips, at the top of the hill five hundred feet away.

She didn't run away when Fukaziroh approached. In fact, she even took a few steps down the slope closer to the other girl.

"Grrr…"

Fukaziroh's pace naturally got faster. Soon they were barely two hundred feet apart.

"What's going on? If Pitohui came back now, she could easily shoot Llenn, right?" said one of the audience members. It was the most natural suspicion about the way Llenn and Fukaziroh were approaching each other.

"Probably, but if she beat her that way, you *know* she wouldn't be satisfied with it at all," said a voice with great authority from the back.

"What do you mean? How do you know that, huh?" demanded the first man, turning around.

"Because I was just fighting with her moments ago," said a smiling David, his camo face paint washed off.

"Good point!" said the man.

What now, Pito? What should I do?

Fukaziroh had answered the provocation and marched forward toward her opponent—a choice she now regretted.

Llenn was waiting for her at the stern of the ship 150 feet away, outlined against the gray sky. Her arm was down; the P90 was pointed at the ground. The way she stood there, silent and calm and confident, was like an ancient hero on some mural.

It would be easy for Pitohui to snipe and kill Llenn now. For one thing, she left the courtyard to pretend to go after Eva, to create such an opportunity.

But a victory not from simply "exploiting an opportunity," but "shooting from the shadows at an enemy who wants a one-on-one fight" was not what Pitohui desired at that moment in time.

And that was a fact Llenn had in mind when she engaged in this action.

"Youuuu! You evil bitch!" Fukaziroh couldn't help but scream.

She couldn't shoot Llenn now. Until Pitohui came back, she'd have to bear this situation with a merciful heart as deep as the sea. She also had to find a way to tag-team the fight to ensure that Pitohui and Llenn were the ones in the duel. That was the obligation she owed her teammate.

And what did she get for it? Llenn taunting her with "What's wrong, Fuka?! Is Rightony enjoying a nice little nap?! I bet he is; he'd love a long sleep in a locker! He's just a naptime gun! A big, fat gun that needs an afternoon nappy-nap!"

Fukaziroh couldn't shoot back with her gun, but she could with her mouth. "Don't give me that crap! You have *no* eye for beauty! And I don't wanna hear any jokes about naps from the girl who fell asleep during class and got taunted by the stupid teacher who said 'I guess sleeping makes you grow'!"

Bringing up the taboo of real-life details was crossing a line, but Llenn didn't falter.

"Says the girl who ditched that class all the time and had to beg and weep for a passing mark, clutching the teacher's ankles!"

"I can't help it that I was on so many dates! It's the tragedy of a girl in demand! And you—"

"You tripped and completely spilled your Indian takeout everywhere! Ha-ha, klutz!"

"Hey! It was my turn to insult you!"

"You gladly ate half my curry with tears of gratitude in your eyes, you starving orphan!"

"That's—"

"You forgot your gross granny bra in the changing room on the school field trip, and the hotel called the school about it, and they had to do an announcement over the loudspeaker, you dumpy-bra owner!"

"But—"

"When we had a party to cheer you up after getting dumped, you said 'I'm all about girls now. *Yuri* is the beautiful future,' and the very next day, you got rejected by another dude, you professional rejectee!"

"No—! I—! Argh! Goddammit, that's enough! Sorry, Pito, I'm going to kill her myself!"

Fukaziroh cast aside the shield in her left hand.

"I'd like to see you try!"

Llenn lifted the P90.

Bullet lines traded places, fixing on their small targets.

They fired together.

The P90's 5.7 × 28 mm bullets, traveling over two thousand feet a second, and the 40 mm grenade, at 250 feet per second—you didn't need a calculator to know which would hit its target first if they were fired at the same time.

"Gahk!"

A storm of bullets left Fukaziroh's entire side glowing red. But Llenn just had to turn sideways to evade the direct path of the grenade. The explosive hit the floor of the deck and detonated about ten yards behind her. Llenn kept firing the whole time.

Fukaziroh's body lit up with more and more damage effects. It seemed like they were focused mostly around her left arm—and then she understood.

Aha! She's going after Leftania!

Leftania still had two plasma grenades loaded, and Llenn was trying to blow it up. That was why she had chosen this distance to fight—and not any closer.

Fukaziroh might not go down easy from bullets alone, but an induced explosion of grenades would do the trick in one shot.

What a nasty strategy! Fukaziroh twisted and exposed her right side to Llenn. A hail of bullets enveloped her, with one hitting her right in the head.

"Gahk!"

Her little body hurtled backward, and her helmet hit the floor loudly.

Gonk.

Suddenly, the courtyard was quiet.

"Whew…"

Llenn removed the depleted magazine of the P90 and moved to extract a new one from her pouch.

"Secret Technique: Playing Dead!"

Fukaziroh suddenly bounced back up as if on springs and brandished the MGL-140 in her left hand, which was supposed to be smarting from getting shot.

A big, fat line extended from its big, fat muzzle right into Llenn's stomach. When the grenade shot out, following the line, it was easy to distinguish its appearance: a bold blue color in opposition to the red line.

A plasma grenade.

At this angle, even if she jumped out of the way, it was going to explode on the ground behind her—well within blast radius.

She couldn't avoid it.

She couldn't withstand it.

So what could she do?

She could only do this.

And if she could only do this, then the choice was simple.

The place was easy: atop the fat line.

All that mattered was the timing.

Like Pitohui did with the shotgun in the switchyard, as long as your timing was good, you could pull it off.

Llenn dropped backward—and kicked up as hard as she could with her right foot.

The tip of her boot caught the side of the grenade, away from the fuse, replacing its flight vector with her kick vector and sending the explosive grenade up and to the side.

It eventually whistled over to the side of the outdoor stage at the stern of the ship and exploded into a glowing blue ball. The stage was already in bad condition, and now it was a total wreck.

"No way!" Fukaziroh's jaw dropped to the floor. She was certain she was going to see Llenn evaporated.

"Now that's more like it! That's the Llenn I know! She's still *mine*, Fuka! I'm the only one who can challenge her—and the only one who will kill her! And eat her!" raved Pitohui's excited voice in Fukaziroh's ear. Apparently, she'd witnessed the whole exchange.

"Uhhh, yeah. You go ahead. She's all yours...," Fukaziroh muttered, crawling away from the scene with less than half of her hit points remaining. "Like I can deal with a monster like that."

The crowd watching in the bar had but one comment on their lips.

234   Sword Art Online Alternative Gun Gale Online, Vol. 5

"She kicked it…"
"She kicked it…"
"She kicked it…"
"She kicked it…"
"She kicked it…"
So did David, who stood imposingly with his arms crossed.
"She kicked it…"

When Fukaziroh fled from the courtyard, Pitohui leaped out to take her place from around the side of a storefront.

"Lleeeeennnnn!"

She didn't have that cumbersome shield anymore. Both hands were wrapped around the KTR-09, steadied against her right shoulder, and firing as she ran.

"Eeyaa!"

This time, Llenn could not kick the bullets out of the way. She ducked down and backed away, barely managing to crawl down the tiers of seats at the outdoor stage.

The 7.62 mm bullets that roared past at Mach speed and smashed into everything around her seemed to personify Pitohui's rage and joy.

"Oh, crap! Oh, crap! Oh, craaap!"

Llenn slid down the rows as she yanked a new magazine out, slammed it into the P90, and pulled the charging handle.

Now she was ready to fight back—but she couldn't stick her head out when any of the bullets flying overhead would be an instant kill. That was the power of the seventy-five-round drum magazine.

Fukaziroh watched as Pitohui ran closer to Llenn, shooting and smiling like she had just spotted her lover at the train station.

"Hrmf!" Then she noticed a large figure with braided hair leaning out from a deck up above. A woman with the figure of a gorilla was on the top deck of cabins on the port side, an oddly designed sniper rifle in her hands. She was meant to be a decoy, but with Llenn in trouble, she had changed tactics to set up and aim at Pitohui.

"Up above, Pito!"

"Haaaa!"

Pitohui twisted around to dodge the bullet line from Boss's shot, pointed the KTR-09 at the source of the line, and shot three times in a single instant. Her reflexes were astonishing. The bullets hit Boss on the arm and leg as though they were pulled by gravity. The third one struck the Vintorez's silencer, creating sparks and knocking it out of her hands. The gun fell in the fore direction, thudding on one of the balconies below.

"Whoo! Nice shooting!" Fukaziroh cheered.

"You monster!" Boss shouted at the same moment.

"Fukaaaa? You can get rid of Eva now," said Pitohui, turning her attention back to Llenn.

"You bet! With pleasure!"

Fukaziroh pointed Leftania at the spot where Boss had been a moment before. That would fire a plasma grenade. The distance was about forty yards, so the fuse would activate. As long as she hit the cabins, it should blow Boss and her foothold sky-high.

Therefore, she dropped her aim a bit, to make sure she didn't accidentally send it into the sky.

Boss peered over the side of the deck as she pulled the Strizh from her waist.

"Ugh!"

When she saw the huge bullet line pointing directly below her, stemming from Fukaziroh's left hand, she realized it would be impossible to prevent a plasma grenade from coming.

If she did nothing, it would hit the underside of the deck below her feet, putting her right in the middle of a blue surge of plasma over sixty feet across. And if she turned around to run, the result would be no different. She couldn't move over thirty feet in just two or three seconds.

"No, wait… I can!"

She placed a heavy foot on the top rung of the railing.

"Yaaah!"

Fukaziroh fired her final plasma grenade.

"Rrraaah!"

Boss soared through the air.

She had put her foot on top of the handrail and launched herself with all the considerable leg strength she possessed.

Naturally, she wasn't jumping *to* anything, just setting herself up for a hundred-foot fall into the courtyard below, but the acceleration of gravity was faster than her running speed by far.

"Are you serious?!" Fukaziroh screamed. Boss jumped right past her perfect grenade shot in midair. If it landed on the deck and exploded, it wouldn't kill Boss now.

But she *would* die on impact.

Yep. Splattered all over the ground.

Fukaziroh rested easy. Boss's jump wasn't going to span the thirty yards it would take to reach her in the center of the courtyard. She wasn't going to pull off some wild, acrobatic body blow from the height of several stories.

All she had to do was stand there and watch as her foe's body smashed flat against the cobblestones of the courtyard.

Farewell, my opponent, Fukaziroh saluted silently, following the enemy's majestic arc.

The world seemed to move in slow motion.

A pale explosion flickered and cast a glow of light against the far building that reflected back to illuminate the falling enemy.

The woman fell upside down through the air, her two braids swaying.

Two eyes staring.

Two arms holding pistols. Pointed right at her.

A gun attack as she fell.

Are you kidding? That's not going to hit me!

I want you to sit down and take notes. If you can't do that in midair, at least listen. See, shooting while in midair is incredibly difficult. If it was that easy to hit targets as you fall, I wouldn't be having such a hard time of things. Do you get me? I bet you don't!

As Fukaziroh went patronizingly on and on inside her mind, a 9 mm bullet flew at her forehead and buried itself into her brain.

"Beh?"

Her helmet was an inch too short to block it.

"Heh!"

Having shot a single bullet in the midst of her fall, Boss slammed grin first into the courtyard, denting in the tiles several inches.

As the grenade explosion dissipated, two DEAD signs appeared at the exact same time.

Brilliant!

M had witnessed the whole thing play out.

"Yaaaaah!"

"Urgh!"

Pitohui and Llenn continued their battle, oblivious to the fact that their partners had just died. This did nothing to overturn Llenn's disadvantage, however.

The storm of incoming bullets prevented her from coming up, so she was still crouched beside the seats of the outdoor theater.

Dammit, can I go yet? Now? What about now?

Llenn prayed that her strategy would be a successful one.

She couldn't see Pitohui, but she could tell her general location from the gunfire. She was very close. Less than a hundred feet, surely, and getting closer.

Sixty feet to go.

Still coming...?

Thirty feet.

She's still coming... Am I going to die here...?

Llenn clutched the P90.

And the whole time, P-chan didn't speak a single word.

The moment arrived for both those on and off the ship.

As the crowd watched on the monitors—the ship stood up.

It had been running full steam ahead, even cut down to 1,100 feet in size, but now the entire cut-off portion was submerged, jolting it downward.

The ship was no longer tilting; now it was standing. From the stern, the belly of the ship was now coming into view.

Massive screw propellers were exposed to the air. They were twenty-five feet long, attached to three hanging azimuth thruster pods. Before they had been churning against seawater, but now they carved only air.

With the loss of propulsion, the ship's speed dropped, but it did not improve the angle. It continued to tilt further, with the first three hundred feet or so under the water now. It was like seeing some enormous beast lift its rear end up into the air.

"Oh... I'm glad I'm not on that ship...," the audience murmured in horror.

"Aaaaah!"

Of the three living people on that ship, the sole man felt himself slipping off the deck, lunged for the handrail right before him, but came up just inches short.

"Shit!"

His last-ditch effort was to hurl his gun, which hung in front of his body from its sling. The stock of the M14 EBR caught on the railing, briefly stopping his falling speed. M made use of that moment to reach out and grab the vertical post of the railing, which was now horizontal, owing to the ship's angle.

"Whew..." He exhaled one second before the bar creaked and broke at a spot where it was rusted through. "Aaaaaaaah!"

M's massive form began to plummet. The sling came loose

from his head on the way, his gun slipping away from him. He fell about thirty feet, upside down, and landed on his back on a large bench built into the deck.

"*Gagrbk!*"

The impact was strong enough to cause damage. In real life, it would have broken his spine and ribs. In the game, half of his hit points dropped—but it *did* stop his fall.

M craned his neck and looked to the fore of the ship—which at this moment was *down*.

"……"

Over six hundred feet below, the gray sea had opened its churning, foaming mouth to swallow the vertical length of the ship. A little stick as puny as a piece of trash fell, spinning, toward the water. That was his gun.

There were abrupt bursts of air from the sides of the ship directly above the waterline. With the influx of so much water into the ship interior, the air trapped inside became pressurized and had no nowhere to go, until the side windows proved to have the most give and shattered outward.

Only 625 feet remained of *There Is Still Time* above the sea, now more of a tower than a ship.

There were only minutes until the entire SJ3 arena was gone.

Even less than a minute, perhaps.

"Here we goooo!" Llenn screamed, grabbing the leg of a chair near where she was crouching.

"Ugh!" Pitohui stopped firing, placed the KTR-09 against her shoulder, and rushed for all she was worth up the slope of the courtyard, which was growing steeper by the moment.

"Tah!"

She leaped at the end, stretching out both arms—and succeeded in catching her fingertips on the lip of the first row of seating in the outdoor theater, the last actual space in the entire courtyard.

With her feet dangling below her and tears of joy in her eyes, Pitohui shouted, "Ah-ha-ha-ha-ha! We did it, Llenn! We did it!"

*　　*　　*

Sink this ship.

That was Pitohui's desire and her goal.

It was why she didn't shut the interior waterproof walls, ran it at full speed, and slammed it into the building in order to wipe out the enemy team.

But the preposterously huge craft was far, far tougher than Pitohui could have imagined or wished for. It stayed strong, refusing to go down without a fight. It almost seemed to be holding the wrath of the dead passengers of its past—and of Clara.

She'd pretty much given up on the idea of sinking it before SJ3 ended, but Llenn had really come through in a pinch with that plasma grenade fireworks show.

With Pitohui's efforts and Llenn's finisher, the ship was soon to sink to the bottom of the sea.

"I'm so glad we were on the same page! You really are everything I thought you were, Llenn!" Pitohui raved, pulling herself up to the lip and peering over it.

"……"

There she saw Llenn, standing on the back of a seat that faced up into the sky, silently pointing the P90 at her.

She saw her eyes.

"Ah, you really are my Grim Reaper, Llenn."

Once Pitohui finished saying the words, Llenn placed her finger on the trigger.

A bullet line appeared, stopping right on Pitohui's forehead.

Then Llenn fired the gun.

There was no hesitation whatsoever.

Pitohui's body dropped without a sound.

She passed right by tile floor of the courtyard, which was now essentially a vertical wall, plunging toward the sea feetfirst.

"Gaaah!"

The hands that had let go of the lip just before she could get shot now grabbed the KTR-09 hanging off her shoulder by its sling and pressed its muzzle against the tile floor—wall—whipping past her face.

Zgakgakgakgakgakgakgak! She shot it directly into the surface. The sparks from the muzzle lit the tile wall as the bullets opened holes in it, until eventually— *Chunk!*

After however many shots, the muzzle actually stuck into the hole it had created and jammed there. Pitohui pressed her feet into the tile surface using the stuck KTR-09 as a wedge. The force of her boots cracked the tile, but her vertical movement stopped.

She had fallen over twenty feet. If she looked up, she could see a leaden sky above the cliff of tiles.

"Haaaah!"

Pitohui began to climb.

A few seconds after shooting, Llenn murmured, "It's over…"

She quietly, carefully walked over the backs of the now-vertical chairs, until she got right to the sheer edge of the deck. Then she peered over the spot where Pitohui had fallen.

"Eep!" There she was, only fifteen feet below.

"Ugh!" Llenn grimaced.

On the port-side passenger cabins of Deck 20, M climbed up the railings like a ladder. Ahead, he could see Pitohui clinging to the sheer wall and making her way up it.

In her hands were two thin daggers she drew from her boots. She was jamming them into the tile surface as hard as she could, essentially climbing with arm strength alone. She looked like a rock climber. The KTR-09 was still stuck in the wall ten feet below her.

Then M turned and looked down.

The remaining height of the ship tower was five hundred feet.

"Take thiiiis!"

Again, Llenn did not hesitate.

She pointed the P90 with one arm straight down at Pitohui, who was climbing up from below—and got shot before she could attack. Pitohui was clinging to the wall by one arm and knife, using her free hand to shoot an XDM pistol.

"Urgh!"

The .40-caliber bullet hit Llenn on the right wrist, a glowing-red signal for damage appearing. Since it was just a pistol round, it didn't tear her delicate wrist right off, but it did numb the nerves and cause the P90 to slip from her grasp.

But the strap of it yanked against her back and kept it from falling farther.

At that very moment, Pitohui fired a second time. And at fifteen feet away, she wasn't going to miss her shot.

The bullet flew straight for Llenn's left eye—but hit right near the muzzle of the P90 as it swung from the sling.

Having saved her life, the P90 continued to fall. The shot had destroyed the metal clasp connecting it to the sling strap.

"—!" Llenn reached out to grab the falling gun but stopped herself before the momentum could carry her over.

Barely an inch from her eyes, a bullet passed upward and almost carved off a slice of her tiny nose.

M watched the pink gun fall. It was a good decision to let it go; if she'd tried in vain to grab it, the bullet would have hit her in the face.

The P90 fell past the now vertical courtyard, missing all the storefront signs and amusement park rides as it plunged down, down into the sea.

The tower was now four hundred feet.

When Llenn pulled back out of view, Pitohui tossed the XDM away. With her left hand open, she could wave it to bring up the command window and hit a button that said REMOVE EQUIPMENT BATCH, PRESET 2.

The next moment, both the empty holster on Pitohui's thigh and the one still holding a gun on the other vanished.

The combat vest that was nothing but an impediment to climbing disappeared, revealing that skintight navy body suit. The headgear disappeared, leaving her ponytail to sway with gravity. All she had left were the pouches around her back with the lightswords.

Pitohui grabbed the knife with her left hand again and resumed the violent, two-handed climbing process.

"Ha! Ha! Ha!" she yelled with each plunge of a dagger, until at last she reached the lip of the seats again. She hauled herself up, leaving the knives stuck in the tiles.

If Llenn tried to kick her, she would use the knives as footholds, grab her arms, and toss her backward—but Llenn was not there.

"Guess she saw that one coming..."

She had withdrawn quite a ways back. To the lowest row of recessed seats in the outdoor theater—which, being vertical now, meant she was actually fifteen feet *higher* than the top.

"......"

She stared down silently with big, childlike eyes and reached behind her back. When her hand returned, it was holding a large, mean-looking black combat knife.

"Come, Pito!"

Pitohui stuck both hands into the pouches behind her back and removed her lightswords, producing two glowing blades.

"Here I go!"

The tower was now 250 feet.

"Shaaaaa!"

Pitohui was the first to move. She raced up the "steps" of the recessed seating easily, despite the much larger size, and started to launch a double-bladed attack on Llenn fifteen feet above.

"Yikes!" Llenn ran away.

She turned on her heel and raced up the side of the row with even greater speed than Pitohui, heading to the left along the backs of the seats facing the stage.

"Whoa! What? Huh? Huhhhhh? Are you seriously running away right now?" Pitohui shrieked, aghast.

"Of course I am! Why do you have two lightswords?! It's not fair!" came Llenn's response.

"D-don't be an idiot! It's a strategic choice!" Pitohui raged, swinging her arms in vengeance as she chased. A nearby seat was sliced into pieces and fell over two hundred feet to the sea below.

By now, Llenn had escaped to the left edge of the stage, slipped up to the very end of the ship, and, as nimbly as a monkey, leaped to the railing and escaped up onto the upward-pointing stern of the ship.

"What happened to our battle?! Lleeeennnnn!" shouted Pitohui, who was chasing her despite knowing that in terms of speed, she couldn't possibly catch up.

"You can't beat me! I have the high ground!" the other girl claimed unbelievably.

"Wha—?! You're going to win by making me drown?! And you're happy with that?! Is that how a real woman fights?!" screamed Pitohui, blades in hand, as she stomped across the backs of the seats. This wasn't at all what she'd heard through M earlier.

"Yes, it is! I changed my mind!"

"Shut up! I'll kill you for that!"

"You've been *trying* to kill me this whole time!"

The tag game of Llenn's monkey perch on the stern and Pitohui's considerably slower pursuit continued for a bit.

Thirty seconds later, two people stood at the tip of the 160-foot tower in the ocean.

They were on the rounded bulge of the stern, on a surface that people were never meant to actually stand on. Nearby, on the white outer hull of the ship was painted the name THERE IS STILL TIME.

One of the two was Llenn.

"……"

She crouched slightly, right knee on the ground, with her black knife behind her back in a backhand grip. Her eyes were narrow, sharp-edged, and directed straight at Pitohui.

There was nowhere to run now.

The other person was Pitohui.

"……"

She stood thirty feet away, both arms holding lightswords, extended to her sides. The pale blue-white blades looked like outstretched wings.

The crowd in the bar could see it all.

"Let's do it, Llenn! It's the final fight!"

"With Llenn's speed, she's got this!"

"Slice her up, Pitohui!"

"Show no mercy, Big Sis!"

Based on the voices, it seemed their rooting priorities were split between the two.

One voice louder and more urgent than most belonged to David.

"Win this fight, Llenn!"

"I'm sorry for misunderstanding, Llenn… You just lured me up here to the only flat space where we could fight. Of course. It's not fun to fight when there are no good footholds."

Llenn glared back at her and said, "To be honest…I was hoping with all my heart that you would slip while climbing and fall into the water."

"I noticed that along the way. It's how I was able to stay calm."

About sixty feet below them, the three giant screw propellers continued to spin, cutting massive swaths of air. Not a soul needed to wonder what would happen if a person slipped and fell onto them. And if they fell and avoided the propellers, they still drowned. At best, if their gear was light enough that they didn't sink, the slow HP-draining effect of the water would get them in the end.

"What we've got in our hands are our only weapons now. The

dry ground we're standing on will sink in moments. Let's finish the fight with the next blow, little traitor. This is the end between LPFM and Team Betrayers."

Pitohui slowly began to walk toward Llenn.

"......"

"Anything you want to say at the end?"

"......"

"Then let's begin."

As she saw Pitohui approaching, wings outstretched, Llenn thought, *I'm sorry. I'm so sorry.*

She was speaking to the black combat knife she brought out in front of her body.

I'm sorry, Knife. You have to die to protect me.

In response, the knife said, "*All is well. I wouldst gladly give mine life for the noble goal of ensuring your survival, good Llenn.*" Its voice was calm and measured. "*Just one humble request. Would you be so good as to give me a name before the end?*"

Llenn said, "Thank you. And good-bye...Kni-chan."

When they were fifteen feet apart, Llenn bounded up to her feet and swung her right arm.

It was *similar* to a slash from low to high—but her palm was open. The knife flew right at Pitohui's face.

"*Shaaa!*"

Pitohui swung her left sword at the knife in midair and melted it into a hunk of metal. The knife that Llenn kept on her belt since SJ2, that had come in handy on many occasions, was dead.

She crossed the last few steps between them and raised her right arm high.

"Good-bye, Llenn."

With the quickest speed she'd exhibited yet, she swung down at Llenn's left shoulder.

Pitohui's long arm descended toward little Llenn.

With her advantage in agility, Llenn had time to put her hand to her side and bring it forward again. Then she twisted, ducked under Pitohui's diagonal slash, and moved again.

"H...uh?"

Pitohui's right hand had vanished from the wrist.

The gloved hand holding the lightblade flew off, slid down the rear slope of the ship, and plunged into the sea.

"Huh?"

Why did my hand get cut off?

Even as her mind grappled with questions, Pitohui's left arm was on the move. She swung sideways toward Llenn, who was rushing around her right side.

But before her arm could pass the front of her body, Llenn's little pink form was leaping upon her.

"Gaaah!" A dull pain ran through her left shoulder, numbing the entire arm below it.

Pitohui toppled backward with the force of the jump, and before her back slammed into the ground, she saw what was sunken deep into her shoulder.

A small, angular combat knife.

A weapon that Llenn did not own.

"H-how?" she gasped without thinking.

Llenn provided the answer herself, holding the knife in as she rested atop Pitohui's body. "I got it from Boss! My teammate! I had it hidden in my empty magazine pouch the whole time!"

"Of course! Brilliantly done!" Pitohui yelled. With the other woman on top of her, she managed to twist the wrist of her numbed hand enough to rotate the lightsword against her own legs.

The long blade of light sliced cleanly through Llenn's shins and Pitohui's knees right below them, as smooth as butter.

Four feet tumbled away, and Llenn and Pitohui screamed together. "Gah!" "Aaagh!"

Their hit points dropped all at once.

Llenn's stopped at about 25 percent.

Including the loss of her right hand and the dagger in her shoulder, Pitohui had fallen to 40 percent.

3RD SQUAD JAM: BETRAYERS' CHOICE (FINISH)

"Just one more…"

Pitohui attempted to swing her blade one last time.

Grrck. Llenn twisted the knife in her shoulder, wrenching it with all her strength.

"Aaagh!"

More damage to Pitohui's shoulder. Instead of numbness, there was agony running through her left arm, and the lightblade simply fell, doing nothing more than grazing the spots that had already been severed the first time.

Legless Llenn straddled legless, one-handed Pitohui. "This time, I'll stab you in the face! And win!"

She squeezed the knife in order to pull it out of Pitohui's shoulder, but she felt a hand close around her tiny wrist. Pitohui's left hand had let go of its weapon and was now pinching Llenn's wrist like a vise.

She also brought her handless right arm over and used her elbow to trap Llenn's arm.

"Wha—?"

"There, I've got you now…"

"Arrgh!"

"I can't believe *you* came to me, Llenn… How proactive of you… I love it!"

"Daaaaah!"

No matter how much Llenn struggled, she couldn't match Pitohui in terms of strength. Not only could she not move her arms, the clamp on her right wrist was so powerful that she was actually taking damage from it.

Llenn's face was directly across from Pitohui's. Without being able to move her torso, she couldn't even bend down to bite at the other woman's neck.

Mixed in with the rushing of the propellers' rotation was the sound of air bursting from the sides of the ship as it approached water, a sign that even their floating position had scant time left above the waves.

"You're incredible, Llenn… *This* is the Llenn I was afraid of… It's an honor to fight you. Now that we're here, locked together in this embrace, shall we drown as one?" Pitohui said, her face twisted with joy, inches away.

"No! I'm not into the romantic-double-suicide thing! I'm gonna kill you and win!"

"Oh? How?"

Llenn had neither weapons nor mobility. "Remember what you said before? 'The one who uses their head in battle wins!'"

She leaned her head back as far as it could go—the only part of her body that was mobile.

"Taaa!"

She swung her own head down. Like a hammer—with super-human speed.

Crunch!

The collision of Llenn's forehead against Pitohui's sounded nothing like two biological creatures making contact.

"Gahk!" Pitohui shrieked over the sound.

Llenn's forehead glowed with the red color of damage suffered, but Pitohui was red on both her forehead and the back of her head. Because she was pinned against the hull of the ship, the impact caused double damage from smashing the back of her skull against hard metal.

"More! More! More!"

Crunch! Crunch! Crunch! Crunk-crunk-crunk-crunk-crunk-unk-unk-unk-unk-unk!

The head-butts started as hammer smashes, but with more and more fantastical speed, they transitioned into a woodpecker's rhythm. With Pitohui's powerful grip holding her in place, Llenn's light body couldn't float away with the speed of her jackhammering.

"Gah, gah, ga-ga-ga-ga-ga-ga-ga, ga-ga-ga-ga-ga-ga-ga!"

Pitohui's grunting turned into a drumroll as the light covering her head grew brighter and brighter. On the left edge of her vision, her HP bar was slowly trickling away. But the damage of the impacts alone was not enough to kill her. She still had over 30 percent of her health remaining.

The real problem of head damage went beyond the numbers,

however. It was the same thing in VR that posed a problem in real life—concussions.

A brain shaken badly enough could suffer damage both temporary and permanent.

"Ha!"

So after many, many head-butts, Llenn drew from Pitohui, and the latter's grip had loosened to the point that she easily slipped away. With both hands free again, Llenn practically flipped backward to get away from Pitohui.

The knife, however, was still stuck in Pitohui's left shoulder. And when Llenn tried to stand up, the lack of anything below the shin caused her to tumble.

"Gaaaah!"

So she had to crawl with her arms. Her hands scrabbled across the metal hull until she reached Pitohui's legs and grabbed them where they glowed from being severed.

"Ll...enn... You really...want me...to...die...by...drown... ing...? You...coward...," grunted Pitohui, who was having trouble speaking from the effect of the physical damage to her brain.

"No, Pito. That would be an insult to you, to the warrior who fought to get to this point."

"Ex...actly... Ah, it finally feels, like my head, is clear... In a moment, I'll get up...and be able to kill you. I can fight...with one hand..."

"Hey, Pito."

"What is it, Llenn...?"

"Before that— Die."

And Llenn used all the strength she possessed to push Pitohui down the side.

Only the audience in the pub actually witnessed the end of Pitohui's run.

When Llenn pushed her, she slid down the rear side of the ship until the angle was too sharp, and then she was tossed into the air and went plummeting toward the water. In an instant before she hit the surface, her body intersected with the path of a churning propeller, obliterating her into a million pieces.

The result was a red mist in the air.

Moments later, the ship sank so that the propellers were under the water, too.

Once back in water, the madly spinning propulsion systems functioned as they were meant to, pushing the ship forward— deeper into the ocean. The last hundred or so feet of the ship above the water sank as though on fast forward. The end of the majestic cruise ship was quite abrupt.

When the ship was no longer visible, only huge bubbles remained.

Inside one of them floated a small pink speck.

Huh? I guess it's not over yet...

Llenn was still conscious, floating on the water. For as rough and choppy as the ocean had been, now it was as still and peaceful as a mirror.

Without any legs, she could barely swim, but with all of her gear lost, this was as light as Llenn had ever been, so she did not sink under the surface. But being in full-body contact with the seawater meant she was visibly losing health by the moment. Her current state was maybe 5 percent.

Is there someone else who survived...?

Pitohui had been dropped on the propeller, so she definitely couldn't be alive.

"Must be M, then," she murmured, resigned. There was nothing to be done at this point. She was going to die within the next twenty seconds. "I wonder if he found a boat to ride in."

"No, there were no boats," said a voice behind her.

"Hweh?" Before she could even turn around, something pulled her up into the air. "Uh, whaaa—?"

"Don't struggle, or you'll fall."

Once she was completely out of the water, her hit points stopped dropping at just 2 percent. Though she couldn't see anything but the dull-gray sky, she had an idea of the situation: M was holding her up out of the water while treading. His leg strength was phenomenal.

"H-hey, M! Damage! Damage!"

"Yeah, I'll run out soon. I'm glad I made it in time."

"But...the championship!"

"I don't care which team wins. Even Pito said it: This part is my duty. Thank you, Llenn."

"Huh? What did I do to deserve thanks? It's the other way around, M! It's because I couldn't be clear and direct that Pitohui jerked us around and kept me from properly joining the betrayers' team!"

"That was Pito's fault," he said. It was a decisive statement, brooking no argument.

"Then...then I don't get it. What am I being thanked for?"

"Thank you for taking the fight against Pito seriously."

The next moment, Llenn's body fell into the water. Her face went under the surface.

"Pwah!"

When she breached the water again, she could see a message up in the gray sky.

Congratulations!! Winner: BTRY!

M was nowhere to be found.

Llenn was floating all alone in the wide, empty ocean.

Time of game: one hour and fifty-nine minutes.

Third Squad Jam: complete.

Winning team: BTRY.

Total shots fired: 68,029.

CHAPTER 18

Everyone's Endings and Beginnings

SECT.18

CHAPTER 18
Everyone's Endings and Beginnings

Llenn was back in the waiting room.

"……"

She scooped up the P90 at her feet and returned it to her inventory, along with its ammo magazines.

The knife was gone.

A floating screen gave her a flashy, celebratory message of congratulations and asked what she planned to do next.

"……"

Wearing a robe now, Llenn chose to return to the bar.

After a blinding teleportation, Llenn opened her eyes on the stage inside the bar.

"Congrats!" Someone large hugged her.

"Mgrfh!"

The embrace was so tight that she was afraid her HP would fall. When Llenn finally wriggled her head out, there were braids in her eyes. That told her who it was.

"Thank you, Boss. The knife really helped me out."

"You're welcome. C'mon, let's have a drink!"

Once released from Boss's death grip, Llenn was greeted by cheers and applause for the champion as she walked through the bar. The enthusiasm of the crowd was so great that it seemed as though, if not for Boss there, they might have squashed her in their midst, hoisted her up on their shoulders, and accidentally thrown her up into the ceiling.

Llenn saw the members of Team MMTM sitting at one table and seeing her off with smiles. Among them was the handsome team leader who had technically been her teammate for a short while. He continued to applaud until they went out of sight.

At another table, a green-haired woman—the one who sniped Pitohui last time—and the handsome black-haired guy who was a girl, who'd given her all that ammo, were leaning forward in close conversation. They had both died in the switchyard this time. Whatever it was they were talking about, they looked serious.

At yet another table, five men she didn't recognize were holding their own private celebration. When they spotted her, they shouted out "OB!" for some reason, beaming happily.

She bowed to them, for lack of a better option, and continued on, wondering who they were.

At last, she was brought to a table with six female players seated around it. They were having the latest of what looked like a long series of toasts.

"Oh-ho! The champion traitor is here at last! So let's do one more toast! Whoooo!"

The pretty girl who addressed the group had her long blond hair down, so Llenn briefly failed to recognize her. Once she got a better look at her face, it was unmistakably Fukaziroh's.

As she once claimed, she had the ability to get drunk on the fumes of a situation alone. She was slugging back virtual drinks in virtual reality—and getting virtually drunk.

"Hey, you! You gotta drink *more*, dammit!"

Llenn had never seen her look like such a wreck before.

The other five were the remaining members of SHINC. Black-haired Tohma, blond Anna, dwarven Sophie, older Rosa, and silver-haired Tanya.

Llenn made her way up to the table of Amazons, plus teensy

grenadier, and took an empty seat. There were many men in the vicinity of the table, but no heroes brave enough to talk to them. It wasn't hard for them to have a nice, quiet conversation.

Once Llenn's preferred iced tea was in her hand, Fukaziroh said, very briefly, "And now, if you'll permit me to give a speech— *Cheers!*"

Llenn sipped her tea through a straw, feeling the virtual liquid quench her dry throat after a ferocious battle. Once she had relaxed a bit, the first question out of her mouth was, of course, "Where are Pito and M?"

Drink in hand, Fukaziroh replied, "C'mon, let's give them privacy today, shall we?"

Strangely, the look on her face was kinder and more serious than Llenn had ever seen from her.

❉   ❉   ❉

In a darkened apartment somewhere in Tokyo with the curtains drawn, a naked woman sobbed, "I lost...again..."

She had just emerged from an isolation tank, her small body and long hair still damp, and sat with her face pressed into her knees on the hard floor, trembling. A naked man, thin but covered with hard muscle, silently approached and held her from behind.

"You did well in there. It was an incredible fight," he whispered in her ear.

"I lost agaaaaaaaaaaaaaaaaaaaaain!" she screamed, putting all her emotion into one long outburst. Then she muttered to the man, "Huh? Were you always this warm...?"

"Yes... I always have been, and I always will— *Gnnf!*"

She slipped out of his loving embrace and slammed him in the stomach. "Saves my fist from getting cold, then!" She repeated the violent gesture a second and third time.

"Guh! Agh! Oh, yes, that's it..."

We'll give them some time.

*   *   *

Once Elza Kanzaki had punched and beaten Goushi's hardened body all she wanted and gotten it out of her system, she spread her arms in the center of the dark room, still naked, and, in a voice loud enough that her neighbor would bang on the wall if it weren't a luxury apartment, shouted, "I'll get her next time!"

"You're still going to try?" Goushi asked in disbelief.

Elza happily replied, "Of course I am! I'll play until I win! Isn't that how games work?"

Monday, July 26th, 2026.

On a summer vacation afternoon, three weeks after SJ3, Karen was lollygagging around her apartment, talking to Saki on the phone.

"Elza Kanzaki has a new song! She just started streaming it online! I can't believe it—she announced it out of nowhere!" Saki's excitement was apparent through the smartphone speaker.

"You have to listen to it with me, Karen!"

As they talked, the phone played the song saved to its memory. An acoustic guitar began to strum. Karen linked the smartphone to her audio system to listen to it there. The lyrics displayed on the screen of her phone as she listened, the singing voice filling every corner of her room.

It was a bright, optimistic song. The guitar leaped about playfully in accompaniment to Elza Kanzaki's voice.

Women, be strong, she sang. *Don't give in to your worries. In fact, you might lose often, but don't feel bad. Don't blame it on being a woman, don't blame it on bad luck, don't blame it on society, but keep standing and fighting.*

It was an encouraging song, aggressive and potentially preachy, but it was Elza Kanzaki's musical talent, clear voice, and gentle delivery that made it so easy on the ears. It ended with a beautiful arpeggio of the final chord.

"What do you think? Isn't it good? Isn't it great? It's 2026! And in this crazy, messed-up timeline, there's a song to cheer on all us women who have to live here! I'm so pumped up!" Saki jabbered into the phone at machine-gun speed.

"Yes, it's really good. It's a very Elza-like song but in a way that Elza's never done before... Thanks for telling me about it; I'm gonna download it right now."

"Gosh, I had a feeling you would say that, Karen! I knew it."

"Gotta be strong," Karen murmured, rolling back onto her bed. In her inner monologue, she said, "I want to be strong, too..."

"Huh?"

"Huh?"

The End

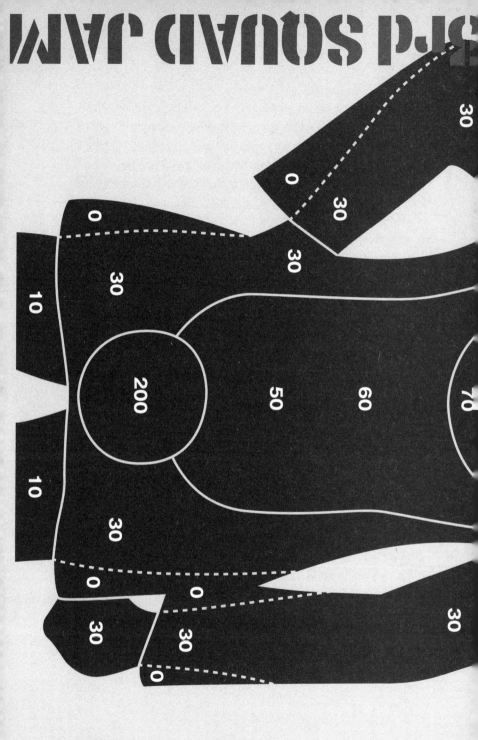

GUN GALE ONLINE

ATTENTION !!
Flip to the next
page to learn
how to play!!

30

100

200

30

AFTERWORD
SUPER-
BONUS

M
SHOOTING
GAME!

GUN GALE ONLINE 3rd SQUAD JAM

AFTERWORD SUPER-BONUS
M SHOOTING GAME!

What You Need

This book
Rubber bands (lots of them)
Hands and eyes
A burning passion for shooting things

How to Play

Open the M target page and stabilize it in a safe place.
Be sure to check around so that stray shots do not cause collateral damage.
Place the rubber band around your finger and shoot it.
Ask your parents for your ancestors' secret shooting style or look it up online.
In any case, find the way of shooting rubber bands that suits you best.
Start from a close distance, then back up as you get used to it.
Shoot like you're Pitohui. You'll feel a natural high.

Score your points based on where you hit
and aim for a new high score.
Pretty soon you'll be going to regionals!

CAUTION!!

> Warning

• Rubber or not, this is a "gun," so do not shoot at
people, animals, or things you don't want to destroy.

• Despite what you might think of him, never
shoot at Keiichi Sigsawa.

• Don't scream or holler, even if you hit a high-
point target.

• If playing at school, do not let your secret crush
see you.

• Don't forget that if you damage the target, the
author would be delighted if you bought another
copy.

• If aiming from half a mile or more, remember
to factor in not just wind and gravity but also the
Coriolis effect caused by the Earth's rotation.

• Don't play using copies belonging to the
bookstore or library.

• Don't shoot with powerful airsoft guns or real
firearms.

Keiichi Sigsawa, July 2016

This is my abstract image of Llenn and Pitohui as a rabbit and a snake.

It feels like they grow more animalistic with each volume. Perhaps by the end of the series, my illustrations will look like this.

Kouhaku Kuroboshi